THE SILVERED CAGE

For an illusionist to make a woman vanish from a cage is merely stock-in-trade, because the woman must go somewhere. But when the woman concerned really does disappear, in full view of an audience, it is the commencement of a baffling puzzle for Scotland Yard. Bogged down in the mists of stage magic, they enlist the aid of the indomitable Dr Carruthers, a specialist in scientific jig-saws, and it is he who finally solves what happened to the woman and explains away the brilliant ingenuity of the vanishing act.

JOHN RUSSELL FEARN

THE SILVERED CAGE

Complete and Unabridged

LINFORD
Leicester

Originally published in Great Britain in 1954

First Linford Edition
published 2005

British Library CIP Data

Fearn, John Russell, *1908 – 1960*
  The silvered cage.—Large print ed.—
Linford mystery library
  1. Detective and mystery stories
  2. Large type books
  I. Title
  823.9′12 [F]   **20021119**

  ISBN 1–84395–855–4

Published by
F. A. Thorpe (Publishing)
Anstey, Leicestershire

Set by Words & Graphics Ltd.
Anstey, Leicestershire
Printed and bound in Great Britain by
T. J. International Ltd., Padstow, Cornwall

This book is printed on acid-free paper

1

The young lady with the extremely pretty face, somewhat ostentatious gold tooth, and innocent blue eyes made no apparent emotional impression upon Detective-Sergeant Whittaker of the Yard's murder squad. But then, Whittaker was trained to maintain a poker face under all circumstances and whatever his inward reaction to this remarkably delectable young woman he took care to keep it under control. Besides, he had a wife.

'I had rather hoped,' the young woman said, 'that I would be able to see Chief-Inspector Garth, your superior. Believe me, sergeant, that is not meant as a reflection upon *your* capabilities, only — '

'The Inspector is away at the moment, Madam. Murder case down in Kent. I'm sure I will be able to handle whatever may be troubling you.'

'Yes — of course you will. For that

matter I'm not at all sure whether Scotland Yard will interest itself. You men of the law have little time for a woman's fancies and fears, I'm afraid.'

Whittaker cleared his throat gently and passed a finger over his crisp, toothbrush moustache. He was a solid, stiff-necked, unimaginative young man, known to his contemporaries as 'Feet-on-the-earth' Whitty. Only rarely did he get an inspiration, and then it was usually something outstanding.

'At least, Madam,' he said, glancing down at the visiting card on the desk, 'your niche in society places you above the average caller . . . '

The visiting card, daintily edged with gold leaf to represent lace, read: *Vera de Maine-Kestrel; The Marlows, West Kensington*. Added to this were three telephone numbers. That 'The Marlows, West Kensington' was sufficient postal address was enough in itself. Vera de Maine-Kestrel was the daughter of Victor de Maine-Kestrel, shipper, banker, chain store owner, and railway magnate, this latter empire being entirely Colonial. In a word, the delightfully persuasive girl with the blatant gold tooth and hat like an inverted pie-dish was worth not one packet, but several.

'I am here,' Vera continued, with a troubled droop of her long eyelashes, 'because I require police protection. Quite frankly, I am in fear of my life.'

'I see.' Whittaker looked at her squarely. 'And your reason for this disturbing suspicion, Miss Kestrel?'

'It's rather complicated.' She made an embarrassed little movement. 'It is mixed up with my fiancé, certain monetary deals, an incident in the past — Oh, lots of things. I surely don't have to explain all those harrowing details in order to get police protection?'

'Not if you don't wish. Suppose we take another angle: who do you think is going to attack you?'

'I can't say. It may be one or several men or women. In my position I am unfortunately the target for many enemies of my father and . . . Anyway, I've always understood that if one asks for police protection it is provided.'

'If the circumstances make it justified, yes,' Whittaker assented, solidly obliging. 'We cannot, however, undertake some indefinite kind of surveillance based purely upon a suspicion. You would have to offer some definite proof. Men are still scarce in the force, Miss Kestrel, and time is valuable.'

'I realize that, of course; but this isn't in the nature of an indefinite surveillance. If an attack is made on me it will be tomorrow evening. I only require police protection for that period. For that matter the protection could serve two purposes, for amongst the many guests some of them may not be genuine and our home contains quite a number of valuables.'

Whittaker did not say openly that he wished she could get to the point, so he remained silent and with a kind of dull interest watched the gold tooth as it occasionally gleamed near the back of Vera's otherwise perfect upper set.

'Tomorrow evening,' she continued, apparently realizing it was time she pinned something down, 'there will be a big magical display at my home, following

4

a dinner. The magician will be Crafto the Great, of whom you may have heard?'

Whittaker nodded. Since one of his own hobbies was a bottomless egg-bag, he kept track of all magicians, professional and amateur.

'Well now,' Vera continued, 'whilst Crafto is entirely above suspicion, I do feel that there is one particular illusion of his which may make things awkward for me. Foolishly, I have already volunteered to be a 'vanishing lady'.'

'Indeed?' Whittaker endeavored to look impressed.

'What, though, if certain enemies took advantage of my disappearing act to kill me, at some moment when I am out of sight of everybody and everything? You *do* understand, don't you?'

Whittaker got to his feet, his usual action when he was not dead sure of himself. Gripping the back of his chair he looked down on the fetchingly pretty girl thoughtfully.

'In brief, Miss Kestrel, there is to be one act in this magical display which involves you in a disappearance. You suspect that may be chosen as the ideal moment to either make you *really* vanish, or perhaps do you a fatal injury. Is that it?'

'That's it!' Vera looked relieved.

'But surely such an attack would involve the magician himself, and I am sure the Great Crafto is an entirely honest performer? Only he will know where you *really* are during this vanishing act, won't he?'

'Unfortunately, no. To make the trick effective he had to reveal its secret to me, and in a weak moment I told my fiancé and some of his friends. I don't suppose they'll betray anything, but on the other hand they might. I want to feel that I have the law present in case of trouble.'

'I see . . . ' Whittaker reflected for a moment. 'Can you possibly explain the trick to me so that if anything happens I may know where to look?'

Vera shook her blonde head stubbornly. 'No. I think I've already said too much. You will see the entire trick performed and if anything *does* happen, well obviously I'll be somewhere in the house.

That's all I can say.'

'*I* shall see the trick performed?' Whittaker raised his eyebrows. 'I'm afraid I shall have to forego that pleasure, Miss Kestrel. I shall not attend personally, but I'll see to it that a reliable man keeps a watch on things.'

'I don't want a reliable man; I want *you*. You're a Detective-Sergeant, and from your very rank alone you must have more acumen than an ordinary plain-clothes man. Or don't you realize that my *life* may be at stake?'

Whittaker hesitated. Had this not been a matter wherein life seemed to be endangered he would have been reluc-tantly compelled to direct Vera to other quarters of the Yard, quarters of the Yard less exclusively concerned in homicide. But in this case there were unusual circumstances. She was the daughter of a rich and powerful man; she was asking an especial favor, and if anything *did* happen to her Whittaker might find himself on the carpet for delegating the surveillance to an underling. Added to all this, he was not engaged on anything of pressing importance at the moment.

'Very well,' he said finally. 'The circumstances being as they are I'll attend the demonstration personally.'

'Not just the demonstration, Sergeant. Come as a guest, to the dinner and everything. I want you to meet everybody — and particularly my fiancé. If anything goes wrong. I'll gamble that he'll be at the back of it.'

Whittaker smiled wryly. 'Apparently your faith in your fiancé is at a pretty low ebb, Miss Kestrel. I'm surprised that you remain engaged to him.'

'I shall break it off before long. I'm quite resolved on that. But let us get this immediate matter straight. Can I introduce you as my friend, Mr. Naughton, an engineer whom I last saw in France?'

'I see nothing against it,' Whittaker replied. 'Providing you do not expect me to speak French!'

'Of course not! You're a solid Englishman whose business as an engineer takes you to all sorts of places.'

'Fair enough,' Whittaker smiled. 'And at what time am I to present myself?'

'If you arrive about six that will be fine — looking the part of course, and ridding yourself as much as possible of that inevitable 'policeman' look which you gentlemen carry around with you.'

'It's a promise,' Whittaker said solemnly, moving to the office door as Vera rose to her feet and picked up her gloves and handbag . . .

★   ★   ★

And, as with all his promises, Whittaker kept it — to the split second. It was exactly six the following evening when he arrived at the great Maine-Kestrel mansion in West Kensington. At first he experienced a certain sense of confusion amidst the guests and servants who floated around him, but eventually he found himself taken in tow by Vera herself, bewitchingly attired in one of the very latest cocktail gowns. As on the previous day, as he was piloted through the labyrinth of the great lounge, Whittaker could not help but notice that gold tooth which kept peeping into view as Vera laughed and talked.

Then he forgot all about this trifle as he was introduced to Crafto the Great. The great illusionist, probably known in every variety hall in the country, broke off his conversation with a gushing middle-aged lady as Vera commandeered his attention.

'Mr. Crafto — meet Mr. Naughton, a very good friend of mine. An engineer. We first met in Paris two years ago.'

'Delighted,' the magician murmured, shaking hands — and as far as Whittaker could tell the illusionist seemed one of the most easy-going and genial of men. He was short in build, wide-shouldered, and podgy-faced. Amazingly immaculate, a stick-pin gracing the center of his stock-tie — a stick-pin with an enormous pearl for its head. The remainder of his sartorial magnificence was made up of an impeccable gray suit with cutaway tails, white spats, and shoes gleaming as brilliantly as his hair.

'You will forgive the unorthodox attire?' he smiled, as he realized Whittaker was studying him. 'For the purposes of my act I always wear this suit. I shall not be present at dinner: That is the time when I make arrangements for the show.'

'Mmm, quite,' Whittaker assented, not wishing to commit himself too far.

'And here is my fiancé, Sidney Laycock,' Vera continued, and almost immediately Whittaker found himself shaking hands with a burly six-footer whose face was remarkable for its squareness and lack of refined detail. Here definitely was a man who would pursue an objective through hell and high water and never count the cost. Anybody more unlike the sparkling, bright-eyed Vera, Whittaker could hardly imagine, but this was no concern of his.

He spent perhaps five minutes with Sidney Laycock, and in that time arrived at the conclusion that he did not like him. He was assertive to the point of rudeness, had an exceedingly low opinion of women, and by and large appeared to view life generally from a very coarsened standpoint. Whittaker was quite glad when at last he freed himself and was moved on to meet other guests, ending with Vera's father, who had only just arrived and was still in his normal lounge suit.

The rugged face of the celebrated Victor de Maine-Kestrel was by no means unfamiliar to Whittaker. On this occasion he warmed immediately to the big fellow's personality — blunt, forthright, and obviously dictated by a sterling honesty. At the very first opportunity he piloted Whittaker away from the general gathering and buttonholed him beside the cocktail cabinet.

'You don't have to pull any false identity on me, boy,' Kestrel said. 'I know who you are, and why you're here. Frankly, I'm damned surprised you spared the time just because of my daughter's crazy notions.'

Whittaker gave his serious smile. 'She is valuable 'property', Sir — if I may use the expression. It might have gone badly with me if I'd refused her request for protection.'

'You believe all that bunkum about somebody wanting to attack her, then?'

'Well, she certainly made it sound convincing.'

'Damned diplomatic reply! You're a policeman, all right! Personally, although Vera is my own daughter, I think she lets her fancies get right out of hand sometimes! Somebody liable to murder her, indeed! It's plain rubbish, Sergeant. Her only object in having you here is so that she can satisfy her ego. It makes her feel important to think that Scotland Yard is keeping watch on her interests. If you like, you've my permission to leave at any moment you want.'

'Matter of fact, Mr. Kestrel, I'd rather stay. I'm a bit of an amateur magician and I'd like to see Crafto's performance. He's quite an expert.'

The industrialist gave a snort. 'No time for such bosh, Sergeant! Making things appear and disappear! What kind of a living is that . . . ?' He broke off and grinned. 'Well, wouldn't do for us all to have the same outlook, would it? See you at dinner. I've got to change.'

Whittaker nodded and, left to himself for a while, took the opportunity to do a little private thinking — and particularly weigh up in retrospect those people he had so far met. Of them all he liked Sidney Laycock the least.

He was still thinking when dinner was announced, and throughout the meal, when he was not answering the most preposterous questions in regard to his engineering activities abroad, he relapsed into intervals of meditation, a habit born of his calling as a police officer. Indeed, he did not really begin to take a definite interest in affairs around him until he was in the great ballroom-cum-hall, where the entertainment for the guests was to be held. He would much have preferred to sit between two people with whom it would not be necessary to talk; but instead he found himself saddled with Maine-Kestrel himself, immensely expansive in his evening-dress and surrounded by the aroma of his thick and fragrant Havana cigar.

'All twaddle, Sergeant — nothing else but twaddle,' he declared, motioning vaguely. 'I wouldn't tolerate such clap-trap for a moment if it were not for Vera wanting it. Hard to refuse her anything, y'know.'

'I can imagine,' Whittaker smiled; then to his satisfaction further conversation was made unnecessary by the striking up of the specially hired orchestra — and from this point the special concert, if such it could be called, got really into its stride, complete with an opening number by the chorus.

'Good job the wife's on the Continent,' Kestrel grinned, as the opening legshow continued. 'She'd take a dim view of my enjoying this.'

Whittaker nodded but did not speak. He was trying to remember that he had come here for a specific reason and that it was just possible that, crazy or otherwise, the delectable Vera might have had very real reason for her request for police protection . . . There was too the quite unfounded possibility that Kestrel himself was doing so much talking for the specific purpose of distracting attention . . . Such were the thoughts that drifted through Whittaker's intensely analytical mind — then when at last the curtains went up on the Great Crafto, he became definitely interested.

Being something of a magician himself, however amateur, Whittaker was more interested in the set-up of the stage itself rather than in Crafto as he made his preliminary tricks to the accompaniment of the customary unconvincing patter. But, as far as Whittaker could see, there was nothing unusual about the stage. It was of average size and bounded at either side of its proscenium by two immensely fat imitation granite pillars. The backdrop was black — by no means uncommon for a magician — as were the drapes to the side wings. On the stage itself there was a table, presumably a trick one, and the usual supply of mystic cabinets and equipment.

There was no doubt about it: the Great Crafto was good at his job. Even Kestrel admitted it, so there was no doubt any more; then after a superbly executed routine with the Chinese Rings, Crafto held up his hand and stilled the applause.

'And now, my good friends, we come to the greatest trick of all — the mightiest vanishing trick ever attempted. I tell you, in confidence, that so far this illusion has not been presented anywhere, not even to the Magic Circle, the proving ground for most feats of the unbelievable . . . What is even more significant, our charming hostess, Vera de Maine-Kestrel herself, has offered to be the 'victim' of the vanishment . . . '

Applause drowned the remainder, and Crafto smiled broadly; then be added, 'Whilst our back-stage friends set up the apparatus I must make a quick change. An illusion such as this demands the appropriate attire.'

With that he bowed quickly and hurried away on closing the curtains. The lights came up and the orchestra resumed its activities. Whittaker looked about him sharply, and finally towards Kestrel himself.

'Should I go back-stage, do you think?' Whittaker asked.

'What in hell for?'

'Merely to make sure there are no characters there who haven't a good reason to be. After all, Mr. Kestrel, I am here to protect your daughter, and for that reason I feel I should take every precaution.'

Kestrel grinned round his Havana. 'Give yourself a rest, Sergeant, and let my daughter's cock-eyed notions take care of themselves. If anything happens — which is about as likely as the end of the world — I'll take the responsibility.'

Whittaker hesitated, then slowly relaxed again. After all, it was no part of his job to snoop and prowl against the wishes of the master of the house unless — absurd suspicion again! — the industrialist was deliberately preventing a back-stage investigation. It seemed hard to reconcile this, though, with his craggy, good-natured face and tolerant grin.

'This fellow Crafto's a good showman; I'll hand him that much,' he said. 'Even changes his clothes to get in the mood. Doesn't mean a thing, of course, but it's good atmosphere. There are even some mugs who believe the clothes might have a direct bearing on the illusion. One born every minute, Sergeant.'

Whittaker was spared the need of answering as the curtains swept back and the Great Crafto was visible once more. This time he was attired in a cloak festooned with glittering stars and crescents. Upon his sleek black head was the conical hat of a wizard, and in his hand the inevitable wand. These, of course, were merely the stock-in-trade of his act: in the main, attention was centered on the apparatus in the center of the stage itself.

Hanging from the flies on a strong, brightly glittering chain was a giant edition of a normal bird cage. It gleamed with the brilliance of silver, though obviously could not have been made of this metal because of the cost. The bars were about six inches apart, bending inwards to join the big hub and clip at the summit, whilst at the bottom they were set into a base about two inches thick. There was nothing else on the stage at all — just this silvered cage, perhaps six feet high, suspended so that one could see through it, under it, and around it. To further satisfy the now silent audience Crafto walked around the cage and was visible as he passed behind it, then he thumped it with his wand to prove the metallic content of the equipment.

'My friend — The Silvered Cage!' he exclaimed, with a flourish. 'Nobody anywhere near it, and our hostess Vera Kestrel least of all. And yet — watch!'

He clapped his hands and a girl assistant brought to him a folded cloth. With a few deft movements, as the girl disappeared again into the wings, Crafto had the cloth draped around the cage and a zipper down its length made sure it could not slip off.

'Lights!' Crafto boomed, and two brilliant limes from high in the flies concentrated their brilliance on the covered cage.

'This chap's damned original,' Kestrel muttered, as Whittaker watched fixedly. 'Most of these gentry work in half-gloom. This stunt's so brilliant it nearly hurts the eye.'

'And now — behold!' Crafto cried. He tapped the cage twice, whipped away the cloth zipper, and there in the cage, clear for everybody to see, was Vera herself! There was no possible doubt about it.

Her cocktail gown was recognizable, and, even more surprising, she was bound about with strong cords. She moved her head and smiled a little.

'Speak to us, dear lady,' Crafto cooed. 'Are you quite comfortable?'

'Roped up like this?' Vera demanded. 'Hardly! But all for the love of art! *I* know how I got into this cage, ladies and gentlemen, but do any of *you*?'

The response to this was a thunderous round of applause in which Whittaker joined. He was so carried away by the brilliance of the illusion that he had forgotten his real task . . . But the end was not yet. Crafto, at the side of the cage, surveyed the bound girl in the midst of the bars, then he waved his wand mysteriously towards her — again and again. The reason for this became apparent after a moment or two.

Here, surely, was the ultimate in stage illusions, for without any covering over the cage, with only Crafto near her, with the cage suspended on its chain two feet above the floor, Vera actually began to *fade!* She smeared mysteriously, vanished in dim vapors, and at length had gone entirely. The bars that had been behind her were in view again, but of she herself there was no trace or sign.

'First class!' roared Sidney Laycock, jumping up and leading the clapping. 'What a pity you can't do that with all women, Crafto! Fade 'em out when they get a damned nuisance, eh?'

'That ape talks too much,' Kestrel growled. 'One of these days I'll kick him out of the damned house. Can't think what Vera sees in him.'

'And now,' Crafto murmured, bowing and smiling 'we bring the little lady back to you, safe and sound, and devoid of her ropes.'

He held out his hand dramatically towards the left wings and waited. Vera did not appear. Crafto frowned very slightly and held out his hand again . . . Silence, and a tension that seemed as though it would make a distinct bang when it broke.

'Vera!' Crafto called anxiously. 'Vera! Come *on*!'

He was no longer a clever illusionist: he

was a much-worried ordinary man. He moved quickly towards the wings, then the chorine who had brought him the cage cloth came in view. Her words came distinctly to the audience.

'She's not back here, Mr. Crafto. We haven't seen her.'

'But — but you *must* have!' Crafto gasped. 'Here, let me take a look.'

He dashed into the wings, and in that moment Whittaker was on his feet, cursing himself for his lapse in surveillance. The tycoon jumped up beside him, biting hard on his cigar.

'What blasted monkey business are they up to with my girl?' he barked. 'I'll soon settle this . . .'

He led the way to the stage, gaining it by climbing the four steps at the side. Whittaker, Sidney Laycock, and a whole host of guests were right behind him.

'Crafto!' Kestrel boomed. 'Where are you? Come here!'

For the moment Whittaker was not vitally interested in Crafto; he was looking at the hanging cage, standing now right beside it. The limelights were

23

extinguished now, but he could see the cage details clearly enough, and there certainly did not seem to be anything odd about it. It was metal all right and, at first glance, there were no signs of traps, movable bars, or anything of a magical nature.

Then Crafto reappeared, pulling off his wizard's hat. There were beads of perspiration coursing down his forehead as he faced the smolderingly angry tycoon.

'Where's my daughter?' Kestrel demanded.

'I just don't know, Mr. Kestrel — '

'Don't *know*! Stop talking like an idiot! You performed this trick and you must know where she is!'

'But I don't!' Crafto insisted. 'She should have been in the wings, ready to come out when I called her. But she isn't. She's utterly disappeared.'

'I think,' Whittaker put in, with heavy calm, 'that I had better take over from here.'

Kestrel glanced at him. 'Yes, maybe you had.'

Crafto waited, still glancing around

him. Whittaker studied him, quite satisfied that the man was genuinely flustered. No actor, no matter how good, could have faked this anxiety of mind.

'Just what is the procedure of this illusion?' Whittaker questioned. 'When we know that, we may have a better idea of how to act.'

'Why should I give away a cherished secret to a complete stranger?' Crafto snapped. 'Who *are* you anyway?'

Whittaker held out his warrant-card, which plainly took the magician by surprise. Just the same his mouth was still stubborn.

'Your being a police officer naturally makes a difference,' he admitted, 'but I'm not giving away the secret of this illusion, even to you. I *will* tell you what should have happened in regard to Miss Kestrel, though. Following her disappearance from the cage, performed by a means which is my secret — and hers too — Miss Kestrel should have been able to reappear in the wings there and then come on the stage.'

'How would she get into the wings?'

Kestrel demanded. 'That is what we wish to know.'

'There is a passage under this stage which leads to a trap-door in the wings. In fact there is one both sides. Let it suffice that she should have passed along that tunnel to the wings — only she didn't, and she isn't anywhere in the tunnel below stage either. I've just looked.'

'Then it's time *we* looked,' the magnate decided. 'Follow me, the rest of you.'

Crafto himself showed no hesitancy over revealing the position of the wing trapdoor, which was still open from his own emergence therefrom. Light was gleaming below and he led the way quickly down the steps into the narrow passage that went directly under the stage. Crafto pointed above his head to the outline of a closed trap set in the stage floor itself.

'That's where she should have come through,' he explained. 'Never mind *how*, but that's the truth.'

'Half a story is no damned good to us!' Kestrel declared, his eyes hard. 'My daughter's gone and I want this whole idiotic illusion explained! Out with the facts, Crafto!'

'No,' the magician replied stubbornly. 'I flatly refuse. This trick is worth a fortune on the halls to me and with the secret gone I'll be nowhere.'

'Since Vera knows the trick already I don't see what you're so cautious about,' Sidney Laycock remarked cynically. 'Whoever heard of a woman able to keep her mouth shut?'

Whittaker was not taking much notice of the conversation. He was looking back and forth along the corridor, putting into practice the powers of observation in which he was trained. Not that he saw anything very interesting. The passage was a normal one of rough brick, and at either end of it were the bases of the two imitation granite pillars that stood at either end of the proscenium. Down here, though, they were no longer surfaced with imitation granite: they were plain brick-built in cylindrical style after the fashion of a factory chimney.

'Well, all right,' came Kestrel's growling

27

voice. 'Since you see fit to be obstinate about this business, Crafto, we'd better finish our journey along this passage to the other side of the stage. Maybe she took the wrong direction and lost herself in the opposite wings, or something.'

Such a possibility was obviously unlikely in the case of a girl as bright as Vera. Whittaker ponderously followed the party down the remaining length of the passage and eventually they climbed the few steps at its other end, emerging into the midst of the crowd of guests who were by now hunting around in all corners of the stage, assisted by the artistes themselves, most of whom had not yet changed back into everyday attire.

'Has anybody looked outside the house?' Whittaker asked, abruptly taking charge as he moved to the center of the stage.

'Madge and I did,' one of the chorus girls volunteered. 'We went right out onto the driveway and had a look round the paths generally, but we didn't see anything unusual. In any case, to get away from the back stage here Vera would have had to pass us, and we were standing in the wings there all the time watching the show.'

'You watched the illusion, you mean?' Whittaker questioned.

'Yes . . . ' The girl hesitated and her shoulders shrugged. 'Not that that solves anything. We're as mystified as everybody else.'

Whittaker made up his mind and turned to Kestrel. 'Mr. Kestrel, I'm leaving it to you to see that nobody leaves here whilst I'm absent. I'm going to ring up the Yard and have your daughter's description circulated immediately. I'm also getting some experts down here to take photographs, statements, and so forth. I'll be back in a moment — and none of you are to touch anything, if you please.'

Definitely worried Whittaker descended from the stage and went as quickly as possible into the house regions. He was decidedly worried. It was rare that the onus rested squarely on him: he was accustomed to sharing it with his dyspeptic superior, Chief-Inspector Garth, but on this occasion the whole thing had dropped right in his lap.

'Whittaker here,' he said briefly, when finally he had made 'phone contact with the Yard. 'Send a couple of men down to Victor de Maine-Kestrel's place immediately — The Marlows, West Kensington: they'll be needed for guard duty. Also a photographer. I'll wait.'

'What about Inspector Garth, Sergeant?' came the voice at the other end. 'Don't you want him, too?'

'More than anything else on earth, but he's in Kent.'

'He *was*. He came in half an hour ago, and right now he's in his office, cleaning up accumulated reports and correspondence. I'll switch you through.'

With a sense of vast relief Whittaker waited, then Mortimer Garth's gravelly voice came through.

'Yes? Garth here. Chief-Inspector Garth, C.I.D.'

2

'Mighty glad to hear your voice, Chief!'

'Why should you be?' Garth asked dourly. 'We don't love each other that much, do we? I got your note, Whitty, about your doing duty at the Kestrel social. Maybe you were justified, but don't be too long about it — '

'I'm ringing up about it this very moment,' Whittaker interrupted urgently. 'I've slipped up on the job somehow and Miss Kestrel's vanished, been kidnapped, or something. It's the oddest thing I ever struck.'

'I'm listening,' Garth growled, and over the wire there came the scrape of a match as he evidently lighted one of his powerful cheroots. Thereafter he was deadly silent as Whittaker gave all the particulars, dressing them as usual in a wealth of careful detail.

'Dammit, man, it's impossible!' Garth

31

snorted. 'The girl couldn't just vanish into thin air.'

'I know that, sir, but where *did* she go? I've tried every line I can think of and not a soul's seen her. Think you can spare the time to come over and have a look?'

'I suppose I might, but it isn't strictly in our line. We are the murder squad, Whitty, not a collection of watchdogs over a feather-brained heiress. I'm not too sure that this isn't in Marsden's province, not ours.'

'With respect, sir, I differ there. Miss Kestrel *did* say she suspected an attempt might be made on her life. Such a thing might possibly have happened.'

'Mmmm . . . All right,' Garth sighed. 'And this is just another sample of my luck. I finish up the Kent business in record time, promise myself a little relaxation, and now I'm roped into this. All right, I'll come over. What's the address?'

'The Marlows, West Kensington. A squad car will be coming in any case, so it'll bring you along.'

The line became dead and Whittaker

returned, in a greatly lightened frame of mind, to the stage, the puzzled guests, and the mystery of the vanished heiress. In the interval Crafto had evidently found time to change for he was back in his impeccable suit, with the stock-tie and pearl stick-pin.

'Did you contact the Yard, Sergeant?' he asked anxiously, and Whittaker gave a grim smile.

'I did, yes. My superior, Chief-Inspector Garth, is coming over. He'll be able to handle this business much better than I can.'

'Whole thing will probably turn out to be a hoax,' Sidney Laycock said. 'Vera's that kind of girl — no sense of responsibility. Completely empty-headed.'

'That's my daughter you're talking about, Sid,' Kestrel rumbled. 'I'm none too sure I like your tone!'

'Well, what do you propose to do about it?' Laycock asked sourly, his sensual mouth setting in a harsh line.

Kestrel hesitated, but he did not say anything further — to Whittaker's vague surprise. He had almost expected a violent outburst from the tycoon, but evidently he was too worried — or something — to make any definite move. So, pondering to himself, Whittaker went on the prowl again, pausing at length beside the motionless cage as it hung from its chain.

'Did you have my daughter's description circulated?' Kestrel demanded, wandering to Whittaker's side.

'No, sir. I was going to, then when I realized the Inspector would be handling everything I decided to leave it to his discretion.'

'And in the meantime my daughter may be getting further and further away! Abducted! Maybe killed! God, how right she was when she said she suspected some kind of attempt might be made upon her life. That's woman's intuition for you!'

'From all accounts she hasn't left the building, so her abduction becomes a matter of speculation.'

'She must have left *somehow*, despite the fact that nobody saw her. I think you ought to move yourself, Sergeant. You're far too complacent about the whole thing!'

Whittaker shrugged. 'It's up to the Inspector now, sir, not me.'

Kestrel muttered something and wandered back to join the still wondering guests and the constantly evasive Crafto. Left to himself, Whittaker studied the silvered cage intently, testing each bar with his pencil — to avoid smudging any fingerprints there might be — and receiving back from each bar a true metallic ring. This in itself was enough to show that each bar was solidly cast and not in any way faked. Every bar solidly imbedded top and bottom? No sign of a door of any kind? Whittaker could be forgiven the deepening wonder that was overcoming him . . .

He looked up at the chain suspended from the flies. Nothing out of the ordinary there. Then he looked to either side of him towards the wings. His gaze travelled over the imitation granite pillars, along the extinguished footlights and above to the likewise extinguished battens — and finally he looked at the closed trap almost at his feet. By what conceivable magical twist had Vera been expected to vanish through *that* with a gap of two feet at the base of the cage?

Whittaker pulled his notebook from his pocket and began to jot down the various observations he had made; then he went on the move again and down into the passageway under the stage. The light was still shining and very carefully he walked along and examined the walls and ceiling as he went, pausing for a long time at the closed trap-door and studying it. Up above he could hear the murmurings of the guests and the occasional bellowing voice of de Maine-Kestrel himself. But that trapdoor . . . There was just nothing whatever peculiar about it.

'On the other hand girls don't vanish into thin air,' Whittaker mused, frowning. 'Or *do* they . . .?'

For an instant he was disturbed by an alarming thought. At the Yard there existed a list of people who, down the years, had vanished under the most baffling conditions. Not only women, but men too. There were dozens of them, the most amazing one being the girl who had walked half way to a well in the snow of a winter's night, and never been seen since! If this was going to turn out to be just such another riddle Mortimer Garth's dyspepsia was liable to become a good deal worse . . .

Troubled by this unexpected remembrance Whittaker continued on his journey along the passage, expecting every moment that he would pick up some clue, perhaps a tell-tale thread of cloth, even the corny clue of a fallen button or cigarette stub — but none of these advantages came his way. Vera de Maine-Kestrel had completely vanished . . .

And by the time Whittaker had 'surfaced' again he found his superior had just reached the stage, accompanied by two ordinary constables, a photographer with his reflex swinging from his shoulder, and Stapleton, the fingerprints expert. Garth himself was looking thoroughly displeased with the situation, hands rammed deep in the pockets of his raglan overcoat and battered trilby cuffed up on his forehead. The stump of his cheroot glowed redly in the corner of his iron-hard mouth as he gazed around him.

'Evening, sir,' Whittaker greeted him, coming up.

Garth's pale blue eyes jumped to him. 'Glad you didn't say 'good'-evening, my lad, because it certainly isn't. I've got the devil's own wind tonight. Maybe I shouldn't have had those peaches and cream for tea.'

'No, sir, maybe not . . . Have you met the people?'

'I've seen 'em and identified myself. Right now I'm just gazing around. It all smells to me like a damned queer set-up, but there isn't anything I can examine until the flash-boys and Stapleton have finished.'

Whittaker nodded, his eyes traveling to the oft-repeated glare of the photographer's bulb and the busily pumping insufflator in the hand of the fingerprint man. Then, presently, these two experts nodded briefly and took their departure. Garth ejected his cheroot stump from his mouth, ground his heel on it, then turned to face the grim-looking assembly.

'I have most of the details from Sergeant Whittaker here,' he announced, 'but there are one or two things upon which I would like to be more specific. You, Mr. Crafto — What is your real name? I've no time for a stage alias.'

'Douglas Ward.'

'Okay then, Mr. Ward. I understand you are not prepared to give the mechanical details of this illusion of yours?'

'Not under any circumstances!'

'Very helpful of you.'

'I'm very sorry, Inspector, but I — '

'A girl disappears because of your illusion and you're *sorry!* You'll have to do better than that, sir, otherwise I may make a charge that you're obstructing the law in the execution of its duty.'

Crafto's face assumed its former stubborn look. 'You can make whatever charges you wish, Inspector, but I do not intend to speak — and since this isn't the Inquisition, you can't make me. I'd sooner spend twenty years in jail than give away a secret which can make me a fortune.'

'I see — which means the possible abduction or even murder of Miss Kestrel doesn't bother you in the least.'

'I don't believe either of those possibilities exists.'

'Why don't you?' Garth asked, his glacier eyes narrowed.

'Well, I — I just don't. It's too ridiculous.'

'I can't agree with you there,' Garth said, massaging his barrel of a chest gently. 'For your information Miss Kestrel was so afraid for her life during the execution of this illusion of yours she asked Scotland Yard to keep an eye on things . . . Even so, she has vanished. For obvious reasons no charge of any kind can be made against anybody as yet, but I warn each one of you that no withholding of information will be tolerated . . . For the moment, Mr. — er — Ward, you can go if you wish, but be at my office tomorrow morning at ten o'clock. I'd like a private chat with you.'

'Very well,' the magician agreed, with

obvious coldness. 'And what about my apparatus? May I take it?'

'You can take whatever tackle you wish but *not* this cage or the cover which you used in the trick.'

'I very much object to leaving my best apparatus for — '

'Whatever secrets there are will not be betrayed,' Garth said sourly. 'That's all for now, Mr. Ward.'

His face sullen the magician wandered away through the wings, glancing back once or twice towards the silvered cage as he went. Garth eyed the watchful faces in the glow of the high ceiling lights and then turned to Whittaker.

'Which chorus girl is it?' he murmured.

Whittaker singled her out, and then motioned. Her plumpish pretty face was troubled as Garth pinned her with his relentless eyes.

'Now, m'dear . . . ' Garth's tone was surprisingly conciliatory, as it usually was to the opposite sex. 'You told Sergeant Whittaker that you and a girl called Madge were standing in the wings during the performance of the illusion and yet never once saw Miss Kestrel, except when she was in the cage?'

'That's right, sir,' the girl admitted promptly. 'When Crafto called for her and she didn't turn up Madge and I had a look outside and round the house exterior generally, but there was no sign of her.'

'Mmmm.' Garth jerked his head to one of the constables. 'Hop out there, Crawford, and see if there's anything.'

'Right, sir.'

'And.' Garth continued, 'you and Madge were in the wings during the *entire time* the cage illusion was performed?'

'From beginning to end,' the chorine confirmed.

Garth put a magnesia tablet in his mouth, rifted silently, and then reflected. The chorine rightly judged that he was baffled but doing his level best not to show it.

'How did the illusion look to you?' he asked abruptly. 'Just describe it as an eye witness.'

'Well — er — Crafto did a lot of wand

tapping, touching the cage to show it was metal. Then he put the cover over the cage and zipped it in position — the cover, I mean. There was more wand tapping and when the cover was removed Miss Kestrel was plainly visible in the limelights inside the cage. She was bound with cords, from her neck to her ankles. Her arms were pinned to her sides. It wasn't a model or anything because she moved and spoke.'

'Spoke?' Garth repeated, and glanced at Whittaker. 'You didn't mention that, Whitty.'

'I forgot it, sir,' Whittaker muttered, crestfallen. 'I was so absorbed in the trick I overlooked that I should record everything. I remember that Miss Kestrel did speak but I certainly can't recall what she said.'

'*I* can,' the chorine proclaimed brightly. 'She said it was all for the love of art that she was trussed up, and she also said that *she* knew the secret of the cage, but did anybody else?'

'I see.' Garth's eyes shifted again to Whittaker. 'Nice thing when a teen-age chorine has to do your work for you, m'lad, isn't it? All right, m'dear, carry on.'

'Well, just after that Vera started to dissolve. She smeared somehow, as though she were made of — of treacle, and at length she'd vanished entirely and the cage was empty. I think she ought to have appeared in the wings after that, only she didn't.'

'Mmmm.' Garth's hands were deep in his overcoat pockets. 'Many thanks . . . Oh, what was Miss Kestrel wearing?'

'A cocktail gown — bright emerald green.' Garth nodded and the chorine wandered off, apparently thankful the interview was over. There was an interval as Garth stood lost in thought, then he glanced towards the assembly again.

'Does that young lady's description of the illusion coincide with what all of you saw?'

Heads nodded and there were mur-murings of assent.

'That being so I shan't need to question each one of you to determine your individual reactions to the illusion. But I would like a few words with you,

Mr. Kestrel — and you, Mr. Laycock.'

Kestrel and Laycock both nodded and the rest of the guests began to move from the stage.

'I would prefer the interviews be separate,' Garth added. 'It is the custom to interrogate in private.'

'We'll go along to the library,' Kestrel decided. 'If I may have permission to see the guests on their way? Obviously the whole social is at an end . . . '

'Do as you wish,' Garth assented, and stood looking at the cage as Kestrel and Laycock followed the guests into the body of the hall.

'Pretty tricky business, sir,' Whittaker commented.

'That's putting it mildly, my lad. Quite frankly I don't know where the devil to start. A clever illusion is baffling enough in itself, but when the 'victim' doesn't reappear afterwards it's plain hell! I'd better have a look at that cage. Must be some kind of fake about it.'

'If there is, it's the cleverest one I've seen. I've had a good look and can't spot any defect.'

Which was by no means enough to satisfy Garth. He moved to the cage and peered at it intently, pulling at the bars and tapping the metal to get a resounding ring. Just as for Whittaker so for him: there was no doubt that the cage was cast in one solid piece.

'I wonder,' Garth mused, 'why the base has two holes drilled in it?'

Whittaker looked, only noting what he had seen before, but attaching no significance whatever to two neatly drilled holes, each about a quarter of an inch in diameter, in the upper surface of the cage base. Underneath the base, facing the floor, there were no holes whatever. The base here was absolutely solid.

'Perhaps a misfire when the drilling was made for the bars,' Whittaker suggested.

'Makers of magical apparatus don't misfire, Whitty. Their very reputation depends on accuracy — and so does that of the magician. No, those holes mean something, but there isn't time now to decide what . . . Right, we've Kestrel and Laycock to question. Meantime, Constable' — Garth glanced towards the remaining uniformed man — 'stay here and guard this cage. I'll see that you're relieved.'

'Very good, Inspector.'

'And when Crawford comes back from his inspection of the house exterior tell him I'm in the library.' The Constable saluted and took up position, then Garth led the way from the stage. In a moment Whittaker had caught up with him.

'Don't you think we ought to circulate a description of Miss Kestrel? This may be one of those clever abduction stunts and if so she can perhaps be identified by somebody.'

'Uh-huh, we'll do that. Remind me to ask her father for a good reproduction photograph.'

In a matter of three minutes, thanks to the direction of one of the servants, they had reached the library. Kestrel himself was already there — worried, prowling, his evening jacket changed for a velvet one.

'Oh come in, gentlemen, do. Make yourselves comfortable . . . How about a drink?'

'Not whilst on duty, sir, thank you.' Garth sat down and mused for a moment, then his cold eyes rose to study the industrialist's powerful face.

'It is not my intention to frame a lot of questions for you, Mr. Kestrel, because at the moment I'm as much in the dark as anybody — so I'll just ask you frankly, what do *you* make of this business?'

'All I can think is that my daughter knew something like this would happen and tried to take precautions. Unfortunately, whoever is back of things proved too smart for the police — or at least for Sergeant Whittaker here.'

'This lot,' Garth said, 'would even have caught Sherlock Holmes napping. I don't think we can particularly blame the Sergeant. This is a job that has been carefully planned, pre-timed, and executed. To unravel it we need to go back to the motive . . . First, then, what do you know about this man Crafto?'

'Not a thing, except that he's a well-known illusionist and very popular on the halls. On the face of it he seems a decent enough man.'

'On the face of it, yes. You don't know if he had any dealings with your daughter before this show tonight?'

Kestrel sighed. 'Unfortunately I have always been too busy to pay much heed to my daughter's activities. I can't recall her saying anything particular about Crafto, except that she'd engaged him to do an act and that she wanted me to come home early to see it.'

'Why? Have you a particular interest in magicians?'

'Anything but. I think they're a lot of damned twisters.'

'Naturally,' Garth grinned. 'They admit that . . . Mmmm, so we can get no nearer concerning Crafto than that. Right then, let's take the next nearest person to your daughter — Sidney Laycock. What can you tell me about him?'

'Only that he's my prospective son-in-law.'

'And you approve?'

Kestrel seemed to hesitate, then he shrugged. 'It doesn't make much difference. Vera is — or was — at an age to please herself. Speaking personally I *could* have wished a better prospective son-in-law, but one cannot have everything. After all, Vera is to marry him, not I.'

Garth glanced at the notes he had made at the time of Whittaker communicating on the 'phone, then he asked another question of the magnate.

'Had your daughter any financial tie-up with Mr. Laycock? Or, on the other hand, had they *both* some kind of connection with a financial incident in the past?'

Kestrel frowned. 'What on earth do you mean?'

'I've no idea, sir; I'm just asking you. When your daughter came and applied for police protection she made reference to such matters.'

'Then I don't understand it. She must have been inventing that story in order to make sure of police protection.'

Whether Garth was satisfied or not was not revealed in his expression. He put his notebook away and then gently massaged the fleshy bulges at the corners of his jaws. Finally he said:

'Whilst apologizing for giving orders in

your own home, Mr. Kestrel, might I ask you to depart and have Mr. Laycock come in? I'd like a few words with him.'

'By all means . . . ' The financier began to head for the door.

'And one more thing,' Garth added. 'Perhaps you could find me a good photograph of your daughter for reproduction purposes? I intend to circulate her description everywhere that matters.'

'I'll see to it,' Kestrel promised. 'And I'll have Sidney sent in to you.'

The door closed and Whittaker rubbed the back of his thick neck.

'In the words of the Americans, sir, we're getting no place — but fast! I don't think there'll be much forthcoming from Laycock, either. Nasty piece of work in my estimation. Quite beyond me what Vera could see in him.'

'I am somewhat disturbed,' Garth said meditatively, 'that both you and Kestrel cheerfully use the past tense in regard to Vera. We've no proof she's dead, and until we *have* that proof let's make things happier by thinking of her as still on this mortal coil, miserable though it may be.'

At which point Sidney Laycock came into the room and closed the door emphatically. As usual he moved with clumsy arrogance, his heavy-featured, sensual face half grinning as though he had just heard a doubtful joke.

'Cross examination on the agenda, I understand?' he asked, finally coming to a halt by leaning against the massive fireplace.

'Not quite that,' Garth responded. 'I simply wish to try and clarify a few details. You are engaged to Miss Kestrel, I understand?'

'Any objections?'

Garth made an impatient movement. 'For your own sake, Mr. Laycock, don't answer my questions *with* questions!'

Laycock grinned and hunched a shoulder. 'All right, so I'm engaged to Vera. What next?'

'When, in the past, were you and she connected with some kind of financial deal?'

'When were we *what*?' Laycock stared with what seemed to be genuine amazement. 'Far as I know we never got ourselves entangled with anything like that.'

'Then you and Miss Kestrel evidently live in different worlds, because she seemed quite sure about it when asking for police protection.'

'She did, eh? I just don't get it. For that matter I don't understand why she sought police protection anyway. Who in the world was she afraid of?'

'That we don't know. She was vague about it.'

'I'm not surprised!' Laycock stirred from his indolent position and for a moment the supercilious scowl deserted his uninteresting face. 'Since the purpose of your inquiry seems to be to define my relationship to Vera, maybe I'd better tell you a few things.'

'Maybe you had,' Garth agreed, thumping his chest.

'Well, then, she and I, although engaged, didn't by any means always see eye to eye with each other. Only we didn't let that fact trouble us. Two strong individualities rarely agree with each other, do they?'

'No,' Garth admitted. 'And hardly an ideal basis upon which to begin married life.'

'We knew that, but something held us together in spite of our rows. Only last night we had a beauty.'

'A beauty?' Garth repeated, puzzled.

'A beautiful *row!* All started over nothing and in no time we were going hammer and tongs. Mr. Kestrel must have mentioned it: he even came into the lounge to see what all the fuss was about.'

'And what *was* it about?'

'Just plain nothing — as I told you.'

Garth did not say that he considered this a deliberate evasion, but it was plain he thought it such. Then:

'And how did this altercation end?'

'Oh, on a love and kisses note, as usual. I have to keep a firm hand on Vera: she's headstrong and I'm the type who won't allow any woman to dictate to me, much less the one who is going to be my wife.'

'You are reasonably sure that the union will come about, then?'

'Of course I am! When we find Vera, that is.'

Garth sat looking at the carpet. 'What is your occupation, Mr. Laycock?'

'I'm a chemist — in business for myself. Here's my card.'

Laycock handed it over and Garth glanced over it briefly. It gave an address near the West End.

'Business good?' Garth asked, without raising his eyes.

'Fair enough, when the Inland Revenue's finished with it. Not that that signifies, far as I can see.'

'Frankly, Mr. Laycock, I am only interested in as far as *I* can see,' Garth retorted. 'And now to something else. Did Miss Kestrel ever mention to you that she had any enemies?'

'Not that I can recall; that's why I think it pretty stupid of her to call in police protection.'

'As things have worked out, not *quite* so stupid, perhaps . . . All right, Mr. Laycock, thanks very much.'

Garth stood up with an air of dismissal about him. 'If I wish to interrogate you further I'll either call or ring you up. In the meantime, I must ask you not to leave town without informing me.'

Laycock gave a belligerent look. 'And what in blazes do you mean by that? That's the sort of order handed out to a suspected person.'

'Right,' Garth agreed coldly. 'I should have thought you'd have seen that *everybody* is suspect as far as Miss Kestrel's disappearance is concerned.'

Laycock hesitated again, but whatever was in his mind did not find expression. Instead he gave an angry look and then went on his way, closing the door emphatically behind him.

'Nice fellow,' Garth commented grimly. 'The sort of man no daughter of mine would ever marry, anyhow — '

He broke off and turned as Victor Kestrel came in, carrying in one hand a cabinet-sized photograph of the missing girl.

'This do?' he enquired, handing it across, and Garth nodded.

'Excellently, Mr. Kestrel, thank you . . . '

The industrialist reflected, his face troubled. 'I hope to heaven you find her, Inspector, *and* those responsible for her disappearance. By this time the poor kid is either dead or frightened out of her wits.'

'We have no proof of either condition,' Garth responded. 'So I should not worry yourself unduly . . . Tell me, you heard your daughter and Mr. Laycock squabbling in the lounge last evening. Why didn't you inform me?'

'Matter of fact I didn't altogether think it was worth referring to. Vera and Sidney have high words so often once more didn't seem to matter.'

Garth handed over the photograph to Whittaker and gave Kestrel a very direct look.

'Right off the record, Mr. Kestrel, is there any reason why the marriage of your daughter and Laycock should take place? Forget for the moment that your daughter has disappeared: let us assume conditions to be normal. Would you still agree, in face of these constant squabblings, that your daughter should marry Laycock?'

Kestrel shrugged. 'As I said before, Vera can please herself. I'd rather not enter into it: it isn't material to her disappearance, anyhow.'

'That's a matter of opinion, sir, when one is fighting every inch of the way to discover a *motive*.'

'I fail to see the merest hint of motive in my daughter planning to marry Sidney. It couldn't possibly affect her disappearance.'

'It could if she didn't intend to marry him and it was her only way to vanish!'

A startled look came into Kestrel's eyes. 'Great heavens, you don't mean that she may have engineered the disappearance *herself*?'

'At the moment I don't know a thing, but it's as reasonable a possibility as any other. It's a motive, anyway, and that's what I'm fighting to discover . . . '

Garth paused and glanced round at a tap on the door. The manservant appeared first, and then the constable who had been sent to investigate the house exterior.

'I'll join you in the hall, Crawford,' Garth told him. 'We are just about to leave anyway.'

'Right, sir.' The constable went back through the open doorway and Garth returned his attention to Kestrel.

'I'll keep in touch with you, sir, and you do the same for me. Your daughter will be found if we comb all Britain to do it — Meantime a constable will remain on guard in the lounge. That cage, and the stage itself, is not to be touched or visited by anybody without police sanction.'

'Very well,' Kestrel assented quietly. 'And thanks for all you're doing . . .'

3

Crawford sat beside Garth in the patrol car as Whittaker drove the vehicle through the night streets back towards Scotland Yard.

'Nothing, I suppose?' Garth asked moodily, dragging a cheroot from his case and lighting it.

'Afraid not, sir. Not the vaguest hint or sign. I didn't just content myself with looking at the paths, flower beds, and so on. I examined the window sills, brick-work, and all the lot. I then went back into the passageway under the stage but I didn't have any better luck.'

'Umph,' Garth growled, or something like it, and drew hard on his cheroot. 'This looks as though it's going to develop into one of those genuinely sticky jobs.'

'The fact remains, sir,' Whittaker said, gazing through the windscreen, 'perfectly solid human beings do not vanish into thin air. That sort of happening belongs to witchcraft.'

'Or the fourth dimension,' Garth snorted. 'There *have* been cases of genuine disappearances which even to this day have defied solution. You should know that.'

'I do, sir. I remembered them not so long ago — but in this particular business I get the impression that it was all studied out very carefully beforehand and then performed quickly and with the touch of a master. It's nothing more than a first-class conjuring trick, probably as simple as A.B.C. when you know the answer.'

'And until we *do* know the answer, m'lad, we've a missing girl to find and a lot of queer people to deal with — referring specifically to Crafto, Laycock and Kestrel.'

'Suspect any of them, sir?' asked the constable.

'Hanged if I know.' Garth looked out onto the lighted streets absently. 'I'm pretty well cornered because of lack of motive. I think, though, that there ought to be a tie-up between Vera Kestrel's talk of some financial deal with Laycock and her final disappearance. If we admit that possibility, though, we are also compelled to admit the complicity of Crafto as well and he struck me as being genuinely astounded by Vera's disappearance. Yet, if she had anything to do with the trick herself, she would have been bound to take Crafto into her confidence. Had she done that he wouldn't have looked so convincingly surprised at her failure to reappear. Further, if Laycock had anything to do with it he surely would have been backstage, or underneath it. Hardly a member of the audience in case anything went wrong . . . And those two chorus girls, who have no reason that I can see to lie, did not see anything unusual whatever. And so the merry-go-round goes on turning!'

Definitely Garth's mood was sour: the very tone of his voice showed it — and he refused to be drawn any further either in spite of tentative questions from Whittaker and Crawford. So, with him in a deeply dyspeptic mood of bafflement

Scotland Yard was reached.

His first move was to hand over Vera's photograph for reproduction and distribution, then he put his own and Whittaker's notes side by side on his desk and brooded over them.

'Have something sent in, Whitty,' he ordered. 'This may be a long session and coffee may keep off the gripe.'

Whittaker nodded and left the office, glancing at the clock as he went. It was now quarter past ten. When Garth said a 'long session' it usually meant until well after midnight. Such is one of the joys of being in the police force.

'Summing things up so far,' Garth said, as Whittaker returned, 'I do *not* believe that Vera Kestrel invented her theory of some kind of attack being made upon her. I believe she genuinely believed that something was going to happen — and I further believe her fears were tied up with this earlier statement of hers that you noted down, namely — 'her fiancé, certain monetary deals, and an incident in the past.' Precious little to go upon, but from its very vagueness it carries weight.

She *hinted* at a motive for her wanting police protection, but for personal reasons did not elaborate. How does that strike you?'

'Logical, sir, logical,' Whittaker admitted, thinking.

'It does not seem, though, that anybody knows what this incident in the past could have been — or else they're cagey and aren't telling.'

'Cagey is right. If the deal referred to was something disreputable, Laycock would hardly own up to the fact — and Kestrel, for the sake of his daughter, wouldn't own up either . . . Y'know,' Garth continued, sitting back in his swivel chair and massaging his chest slowly, 'I just cannot escape the impression that there was a vital reason for the intended marriage of Vera and Laycock — and I don't mean a romantic one either. Two people so utterly at outs with each other would not, I submit, marry without some strong motive. Perhaps a business one, or equally possible, the need for them to keep a secret together.'

'Meaning maybe the financial one, or

64

the mysterious incident in the past?'

'Exactly.' Garth paused as the sandwiches and coffee were brought in, then he continued, 'Apart from the immediate mystery of Vera's disappearance we need to know more about that incident in the past of which she spoke, but how to get at it is a stiff one. Laycock is probably the only one with the answers and he certainly won't say a word. What we might do to try and knock some sense into things is examine our own records and see if we have anything on tap which might point to a financial scandal, or something, involving Vera Kestrel, or if not her specifically then the Kestrel family in general.'

'Long shot, sir,' Whittaker commented dubiously, handing over the sandwiches.

'Dammit, man, I know that! When you can't pin down anything immediate the only solution *is* a long shot. First thing tomorrow make a detailed search of the records and see what you can find.'

Whittaker nodded and waited for the next. At this point, however, Garth dropped this particular line of speculation and instead turned back again to his notes. Presently he pushed them to one side and picked up the photographs that had been taken on the Kestrel stage. In deep thought, drinking coffee at intervals, he studied the photographs one by one.

'Just doesn't tell us a darned thing,' he sighed at length. 'I'd swear by everything I've got that no living person could possibly get out of that cage!'

'So would I, sir — which automatically suggests that nobody was ever *in* it.'

Garth's eyes slitted. 'Say that again! It sounded like one of your rare flashes of genius.'

'No genius about it, sir,' Whittaker grinned. 'Plain logic, isn't it? If nobody can get out of the cage, they can't get into it, either.'

'Yes, but . . . ' Garth rumbled amazingly and smote his chest. 'What about the audience, the chorus girls, and Uncle Tom Cobleigh and all? They saw Vera in the cage and she spoke as well. Even *you* did!'

'Looked like it,' Whittaker admitted, chewing slowly.

'Very well, then. You're not suggesting a case of mass hypnosis, are you? That maybe Crafto mesmerized everybody into thinking they saw Vera there when she actually wasn't?'

'I'm not suggesting anything, sir. I don't know the why or the how. I'm stating a logical fact and further than that I can't go — at present.'

'Fairies at the bottom of the garden,' Garth growled, and whipped up the fingerprint report. He read it through, studied the comparison prints, and then snorted. 'Gets better as it goes on! Only prints on the cage are those of Crafto himself, checked by the prints on the wand he used! All that monkey business and only *his* prints! What kind of a quagmire have we landed in this time?'

'Wasn't one of those projection stunts, I suppose?' Whittaker mused. 'Like the one in the Hewlett case? No, couldn't be that. Powerful limelights would blind anything in the way of projection.'

'Mmmm, limelights,' Garth murmured, staring in front of him. 'I'd overlooked them for the moment. Why the stress of limelight, I wonder? A trick of that sort is usually performed in gloom — and the gloomier the better.'

'That was my reaction, sir, too. My only answer to it is that Crafto, to look doubly wonderful, performed everything in the most brilliant light possible — And got away with it, too!'

'It didn't seem to you, did it, that the limelights perhaps *masked* something in or around the cage? A powerful beam of light is quite a smoke screen sometimes when you try and see through it.'

Whittaker shook his head. 'Everything was perfectly visible, which I am afraid only serves to make things more puzzling than ever.'

Garth returned his attention to the fingerprint report; then he gave a little frown.

'I wonder,' he muttered, 'why Crafto's fingermarks are far more prolific on bar number five — counting them from the two holes in the cage base — than on any of the other bars? According to this report they're repeated time and again.'

Whittaker thought this one out with his

habitual calm; then he gave a shrug. 'Logically, sir, bar five has a reason for being handled more than the others. Maybe we should go back and have a look at it.'

'We will, but not tonight. I've had enough for one day and no good ever came of working the human machine to the point of exhaustion. I'll arrange for the relief constable and then I'm going home to bed. You do as you like. For the moment we've done all that can be reasonably expected of us and I can soon be called on the 'phone at home if anything special breaks.'

And, to Garth's intense discomfiture, something *did* break, towards five in the morning. He emerged from slumber to the realization that the 'phone was ringing stridently. Grumbling to himself he struggled into a sitting position and his wife murmured something in her sleep.

'Garth here,' he said sleepily, switching on the bed-light.

'Divisional-Inspector Harris here, sir. I've just been called in to a business that looks suspiciously to me like murder.'

Harris was on the West-Division area and therefore within Garth's particular homicide territory.

'Can't it wait until a respectable hour?' Garth sighed. 'You can get all the reports and particulars and let me have them — just as you usually do.'

'Normally I'd do that, sir, but I think this may have a special interest for you.'

'Why?' Garth forced himself to become attentive.

'You've issued a photograph of Vera de Maine-Kestrel to all police branches and headquarters: and with the photo you said the girl vanished during an illusion performed by one Crafto the Great, otherwise Douglas Ward.'

'Well?'

'The murdered man is Crafto!'

Garth held, the 'phone tightly for a moment, then with his jaw muscles bulging, and the 'phone still in his hand, he slid out of bed, sitting on the edge of it.

'Did you say *Crafto*?'

'Alias Douglas Ward. He lives in a boarding house run specially for pros.

70

The landlady was awakened towards three this morning by him shouting for help and making the devil of a row as he apparently tumbled around the floor. When she broke into the room — or rather her husband did — Crafto was lying out cold. Dead as a herring. Squad car was called and then I was sent for ... I can't made head or tail of the business myself.'

'Place been photographed, finger-printed, and gone over?' Garth asked shortly.

'Yes, sir; all that's done. I can explain easier if you'll come over.'

'I will — immediately. What's the address? Whittaker knows it but I don't.'

'Eighteen Viaduct Terrace, West.'

Garth put down the 'phone, muttered a brief explanation to his half-aroused wife, and then he was in the midst of dressing. In half-an-hour his private car had whirled him to Viaduct Terrace and he clumped up the stairs to the room where the Divisional-Inspector and a sergeant were waiting for him.

'Evening, sir.' Harris saluted smartly.

'There he is, just as we found him. He's been gone over and photographed in the usual positions.'

Garth was silent, hands deep in his overcoat pockets, all the sleep by now jolted out of him. The room was comfortably furnished — for a bedroom — and the bed itself had not been slept in. Crafto was dressed exactly as he had been at the social, in his immaculate gray suit with the cutaway tails, stock-tie, and pearl stick-pin. He lay face up, his expression twisted in the manner of one who has endured an intolerable moment prior to death.

'Peculiar smell in here,' Garth commented, sniffing and looking about him.

'Darned sight worse when we arrived,' Harris said. 'And the landlady told us the smell of it nearly choked her when she had the door broken open. Window's open wide, you notice. We did that, but the smell still lingers. Gas of some sort, I'd say — and pretty lethal.'

Garth nodded, trying to place the odor, and failing. Then his eyes moved back to Crafto as he lay on the floor. Garth noticed something now that had escaped him before and he went down on his knees quickly.

'Any ideas on that?' he asked, and pointed to the dead man's stick pin. The big pearl which had been on its summit was now only a cracked shell, tiny jagged portions of it still cemented into the pin itself.

'I noticed it,' Harris said, 'but I don't attach any importance to it. The obvious explanation is that Crafto here tugged at his collar and stock when he found he needed air, and in doing so smashed the pearl on his stick pin.'

'In that case it's odd that he didn't manage to open his collar or open this stock-tie,' Garth said, and with one easy movement he detached the stock, and the pin, all in one movement. The thing was a ready-made fake on the same lines as a ready-set bow-tie.

It was plain that Harris was not interested enough to consider the smashed pearl any further for he continued:

'I had Dr. Aston do the initial check-up

and he's quite convinced that Crafto was murdered by poison gas. He'll know better when he's made a full post-mortem. There are no other signs of attack on Crafto's person. Somehow he was gassed, and that is where the riddle comes in. The door and window were both locked and there were no signs whatever of anybody having entered. No gas fire, either, by the pipe of which a lethal type of gas might have been introduced. According to the landlady, all the main windows and doors of this place have a burglar alarm system so anybody getting in would have been detected immediately.'

Garth was silent, absorbing the details.

'And suicide is ruled out,' Harris finished. 'No man who is in the midst of committing suicide bangs on the door for help, unless he's got frightened when he realizes he's finished. But if that were the case he'd have a bottle or container of some kind near him containing the gas, and there wasn't anything at all. Place has been toothcombed, sir, and there just isn't an answer. I'd thought perhaps of some disused gas pipe leading into this room, but there's no sign of one. That's why I called on you: I freely admit I don't know how the thing has been done.'

Neither did Garth, but he did not admit the fact. He went on a prowl of the room, looked at the bed that had not been slept in, considered the ceiling, and so finally came back to where the Divisional-Inspector was standing.

'Did the fingerprint boys find anything?'

'Plenty of prints, but as far as they could tell without the normal microscopic examination they all belong to Crafto himself. What other prints there may be will doubtless tally with those of the landlady. I think we can take it for granted, sir, that nobody entered this room to finish off our unfortunate friend here.'

'And suicide isn't logical . . . Mmmm.' Garth stroked the bulges at the sides of his jaws, reflected, then at length moved to the nearby tall-boy, the only article of furniture present which had drawers. He opened each drawer in turn and studied the contents within. Mostly clothes.

'If you're looking for his personal effects, sir, I have them all here,' Harris said, and a nod to the Sergeant was enough for a suitcase, marked 'The Great Crafto', to be produced from beside the washstand.

'Been through 'em?' Garth questioned.

'Not yet, sir. There is correspondence, bills, and odds and ends that may throw some light on the situation. You'll be taking charge of them yourself now, I suppose?'

Garth nodded and glanced towards the Sergeant. 'Take the case down to my car, Sergeant, if you please.'

The Sergeant departed and Garth gave a final glance around the room.

'Nothing for me to gain just standing here and gazing,' he said finally. 'Put a man on duty and have the body removed for post-mortem. I'll check on the reports and then act as I see best. If I need your help I'll get in touch with you.'

'Right, sir.

'I'll take this as well,' Garth added, picking up the stock tie and pin from where he had laid it. 'For some reason this broken pearl interests me . . . '

And so he went on his way gloomily, and feeling very much as though he had lost a good deal of sleep. Yawning considerably he drove back home, but even so he did not catch up on his repose: his mind was far too active. It had been bad enough to have Vera de Maine-Kestrel vanish without a reasonable explanation, but to have the illusionist himself wiped out, *also* without a reasonable explanation, was too much. This was one of those moments which made Garth inclined to consult a calendar to find out how much longer he had to go before he could retire.

When he arrived at his office carrying Crafto's suitcase he was by no means surprised at the polite stare of enquiry from Whittaker as he stood by the desk arranging the various reports and correspondence into neat stacks.

'Been on the job early, sir?' he asked, smiling.

'Enforcedly, yes.' Garth put the case down. 'And from the sound of your voice you know already about our friend Crafto.'

'I do, sir, yes. There's a report here about him from Divisional-Inspector Harris for your especial attention. Also a p.m. report on Crafto's body.' Whittaker sighed. 'This definitely makes things a lot worse for us. I'd rather hoped that Crafto could be forced into telling us something about Vera Kestrel. Now that's wiped out.'

Garth went to his desk and sat down. He took a dyspepsia pill thoughtfully, belched, and then lighted a cheroot. These morning preliminaries complete he dragged the reports to him and read them through. The photographs of the dead magician also took his attention for several moments, then he turned to the p.m. statement by Dr. Aston.

Re DOUGLAS WARD, DECEASED
POST MORTEM REPORT

In assessing the cause of death I am inevitably led to the conclusion that it was from asphyxia, probably created by a lethal gas. An examination of the blood does not show any identifiable traces of the gas, possibly because there was so little of it. The same may be said of the lungs. It is possible, however, that in the case of an extremely potent gas one or two inhalations would be enough to kill a man, and such appears to be the case here. There is no other explanation for the cause of death since the body is in no way diseased and the heart is normal.

GEOFFREY ASTON, SURGEON-IN-CHARGE.

'A gas which apparently came from nowhere and was not delivered by anybody,' Garth sighed. 'You've seen this report, Whitty?'

'I have, sir, yes, and I'm afraid I'm no wiser than you are. Only thing I can imagine is suicide, Crafto being afraid of what might happen to him following the disappearance of Vera Kestrel. He had an appointment here this morning with you, remember. Maybe it got him down.'

Garth shook his head. 'It wasn't suicide, Whitty. Harris got the right angle on that. A deliberate suicide doesn't cry for help when he knows he's dying. He goes through with it, with an almost fanatical determination. No, this is *murder*, and perhaps in one way it does narrow the circle down somewhat in that we have to look for somebody else at the root of this whole damnable business. Somebody preferred Crafto out of the way.'

'Sidney Laycock?'

'Could be. Or Kestrel. Or even Vera Kestrel. Take your pick, because at this juncture one is as likely as another. Dammit, we're not even sure that gas *was* the cause of death: it's little better than a theory at the moment. Not that that matters so much. Our worry is how it was administered.'

'Which, added to the disappearance of Vera Kestrel, is more than enough responsibility,' Whittaker sighed. Then he became his matter-of-fact self again. 'Shall I get these statements typed out, sir? Concerning Crafto's death?'

'Might as well,' Garth assented gloomily. 'I suppose there isn't anything in concerning Vera? Nobody spotted her?'

'Not a word from anywhere, sir.'

Garth dragged hard on his cheroot and lost himself in speculations. Whittaker, knowing this was one of those moments when one was better keeping quiet, went across to his corner and began to type out the statements. When he next glanced across at Garth he beheld him in the midst of sorting out the various effects contained in Crafto's suitcase.

In the main, as Harris had said, they comprised bills and correspondence, neither of which were of any particular help. The bills were chiefly for magical equipment from a well-known London firm of suppliers, but there was at least one separate bill that caught Garth's attention. It was from a London firm of engineers — not in a particularly big way to judge from the memo heading — and said simply:

To supplying One Cage to Specification — £500.00.

Garth reached to the telephone, dialed

the number of the engineers concerned, and then waited. In a moment or two he was through.

'C.I.D. Metropolitan Division — Chief-Inspector Garth,' he explained briefly.

'Am I talking to the proprietor of the firm?'

'You are, Inspector, yes. Can I help you?'

'It's possible. Have you read in this morning's papers of the suspected murder of one Douglas Ward, alias the Great Crafto?'

'Yes — with particular interest. We once did a special job for him — '

'Was it a cage?' And as there was a prompt assent Garth continued: 'That's why I'm ringing you. It may help us in our rather involved inquiries. Can you recall if there was anything unusual about the cage you manufactured?'

'Unusual? How *unusual*?'

'Had it any gadgets or gimmicks? Was it in any way a trick cage? Being made for a magical stunt I suspect that it may have been peculiar in some way.'

'Not as far as I remember,' the engineer

answered. 'If you can wait a moment I still have the original drawing and specification which Mr. Ward gave us — '

'I'll do more than that. I'll take charge of that right away. I'll send a man round for it immediately.'

And Garth wasted no more time in giving his orders. In consequence he had the design of the mystery cage before him in a matter of fifteen minutes and, in every particular it was a design identical with the finished product hanging over the Kestrel stage. The difference here was that each section was fully described for the benefit of the engineers. Thus, the base was two inches thick, and hollow, to be perforated with two holes a quarter of an inch in diameter. Each bar with the exception of the one marked 'X' was to be solidly cast in base and top of the cage.

Garth immediately began scratching amidst his papers and finally yanked up his notebook. He grinned momentarily to himself and then jerked his head to Whittaker as he looked up to catch his eye.

'Come here a moment, m'lad. Maybe

I've got something.'

Whittaker came over quickly and watched Garth's knobbly fingers point to bar 'x' on the sketch. Then he listened to what Garth had to say.

'The fingerprint report says Crafto's prints were repeated in profusion on what I have called Bar five — starting from this first hole. Bar five is also bar 'x' in the specification, and it is different from all the others. Now, listen to the exact specification for Bar 'x'. The bar marked 'x' shall be made of hollow metal after the fashion of an organ pipe, allowance being made at the points indicated for the side of the pipe to open on a hinge. Precision work must be applied here for the hinged portion to lie absolutely flush with the rest of the pipe when it is in the closed position.'

'And that was the one with which Crafto fiddled the most, eh?' Whittaker narrowed his eyes and gently fingered his moustache. 'Whilst I admit it's interesting to find that this one bar is peculiar, in that it is hollow with a hinged side, I don't see it helps us much. The rest of the cage is cast nearly in one piece, which makes Vera's escape more impossible than ever.'

'That's it, look on the dull side!' Garth snorted.

'Sorry, sir. Just the logical approach that's all. At any rate it seems to show that Vera was not in the cage. If it is as solid as this specification suggests, and presumably it is, she could not possibly have squeezed in between the bars — or out. And she certainly couldn't have hidden in that one hollow bar.'

'That's not funny,' Garth snapped, thumping his chest and rumbling heavily. 'Fact remains we've got a faint gleam of light in the blackness. Later we'll take another look at that cage. I want to examine the rest of these effects yet.'

Whittaker nodded and went back to his typing. Thereafter there was silence for a while as Garth continued his examination of the late magician's letters and bills. But that which he sought did not turn up — a letter or some communication from Vera Kestrel wherein she had asked Crafto to perform his illusion. Perhaps he had been shrewd enough to destroy all such correspondence as it had reached him . . .

There was however a clue of a different kind, and it lay in Crafto's bank passbook. An entry for a month before was credit in the sum of £2000 per Vera de Maine-Kestrel. Apparently the amount had been transferred from one bank to another without the medium of a check, a quite normal procedure in the case of a woman as moneyed as Vera.

'But it doesn't tell us anything,' Garth sighed, and Whittaker wondered vaguely what he was talking about. 'It could be a quite legitimate fee for Crafto giving his show: it could be hush money for a shady transaction such as arranging her disappearance. We just can't find out because Vera's missing and Crafto's dead. Hell's bells, this is a stinker!'

'Yes, sir,' Whittaker agreed, and went on typing.

'And reverting back to Crafto,' Garth resumed, after a moment, 'does it occur to you that he was fully dressed when he was found dead at three o'clock in the morning? I wonder where he'd been until that hour? He left the Kestrel place around nine — yet it must have taken him all that time to get back to his rooms. Did he check up on Vera, I wonder? Even visit her?'

'We're not likely to know the answer to that, sir.'

Garth stubbed out his cheroot in the ashtray and got to his feet.

'We've wasted enough time mulling over reports that don't do us any good, Whitty. We're going to take another look at that cage at the Kestrel's. Let's be moving.'

In fifteen minutes they were there, the relief constable seated on a chair on the stage reading a magazine. He came to attention swiftly as he realized Garth and Whittaker were approaching.

'All right, man, get on with your reading,' Garth growled. 'I'm no tyrant. Anything happened? Anybody been?'

'Nothing whatever, sir. Mr. Kestrel looked in this morning before leaving for business, and he asked the same question as you.'

'No strange sounds of any sort?'

The constable gazed woodenly. 'No, sir.

Nothing like that.'

With a nod and his brow furrowed Garth wandered away to the stage center and considered the cage. Then he glanced about him.

'Oughtn't there to be a couple of limelights to liven things up around here? I can't see what the blazes I'm doing!'

'I'll locate them, sir,' Whittaker promised and hurried away.

Meantime Garth wandered about the stage, kicking gently at the walls, pulling at the drapes, but none the less finding everything in perfect order, It was the abrupt appearance of intense white light which brought him back to the cage. Now there was no difficulty in seeing it in every detail, including Bar five.

Carefully, Whittaker presently returning to his side, Garth tested the solitary bar, fingering and fumbling until at length the side of it snapped open abruptly on a concealed spring. Inside the tube, at top and bottom of the opened slot, was a small upraised knob, a metallic nipple, and each was of identical size. And that was all.

'Some help that is,' Garth muttered at last, closing the side of the tube up again. 'Doesn't make sense in any language. Just as helpful as these two holes in the cage base which don't mean a thing.'

He looked at the holes carefully in the intense light, even using his lens, but they did not reveal anything of interest.

'Yet I *know* they're intended for something,' Garth insisted. 'Otherwise why put them there? Certainly can't be intended for ventilation — Hell!' he broke off, rubbing the back of his neck.

'What, sir'?' Whittaker asked, surprised.

'These limelights! They're the hottest I've felt in many a long day!'

4

Since he was not in a direct line with them Whittaker had not noticed the intense heat of the limes — but now he thrust his hands into the beams he distinctly noticed that they were hot beyond the average.

'Something odd about those limes,' Garth said abruptly. 'I'll swear they oughtn't to be *that* hot Let's take a look at 'em.'

'Bit of a climb, sir. They're up in the flies and automatically lighted by a switch on the main board at the back wall there.'

'I'm not so ancient I can't climb a ladder,' Garth grunted, turning. 'Lead the way.'

Whittaker did so and in a moment or two, watched with interest by the guardian constable below, they had both reached the small but strong platform where the righthand limelight was standing. In actual fact it was a baby-spot of the latest type. Cautiously Garth reached out and touched the top of the lamp-house, then he jerked back his fingers and swore.

'Hot as Hades! And we can gamble the other one will be in a similar condition. Get down and switch 'em off, Whitty. Give 'em time to cool. Switch on the first battens instead, then we can see what we're doing.'

Whittaker descended again actively and, whilst he waited, Garth surveyed the flies from his exalted position. After a moment or two he frowned and gazed intently at what looked like a ventilator grating fixed in the roof. Nothing unusual about that, of course, but it did strike him as more than passing strange that in a little theatre so beautifully fitted up — almost everything being new — this particular grating should have a hole smashed in its gilt filigree. Not a big hole — no more than three inches at its narrowest point and perhaps six at its widest. The broken filigree ends were bent upwards, as though a blow had come from below.

At which point the limelights expired and the battens came up. So did Whittaker — to have the broken ventilator grid pointed out to him.

'I suppose it *is* a bid odd, sir,' he confessed.

'No doubt of it, in a place as well got up as this one.'

'You're not suggesting, sir, are you, that maybe Vera went through there. She wasn't so very slim — '

'I'm not suggesting anything so damned cockeyed! But *something* had gone through there — from below, otherwise the broken ends would not be pointing upwards. While these lamps cool off we might as well take a look in the false roof.'

The entrance to the false roof took a bit of finding but it was located eventually, and they ascended into an immense space that smelt of dust and dry wood. A light switch beside the trap that gave ingress brought into being a powerful 500-watt lamp, more than sufficient for them to behold the details of this big empty area between the ceiling of the theatre-cum ballroom, and the roof proper.

Balancing on the narrow wooden track that led to the cisterns and cooling system, Garth eventually came to the ventilator grid and studied it thoughtfully. It was not — as it had appeared from a distance — made of metal but of thin gilded wire. Under the slight pressure he applied the wire bent easily. All very interesting, but it did not *tell* anything.

Frowning, he looked below. From his position he could see the back of the swinging cage and part of the black draped wall to the rear. The solitary constable was visible too, returned by now to his magazine. For a moment a thought stirred in Garth's mind, but it had gone again before he could catch it.

Since he could get nothing out of this particular angle he turned his attention to the chain of the cage. It came upwards through a hole in this false roof and was fastened thereafter to a winch. Evidently — since he had no assistants — Crafto had set the cage himself and operated the winch. All right. Nothing phenomenal about this either . . .

'Nothing stirs in my addled brain,' Garth sighed. 'And I'll get the devil's own wind if I stay cramped like this much longer. Let's have another look at those spotlights.'

So they began to return to their former position, until Whittaker gave them pause and pointed.

'What do you suppose those round tops are for, sir?'

It was a moment or two before Garth grasped what was meant when he saw that at opposite ends of this wide space, conforming with the position of the imitation granite pillars at either side of the stage, there were what appeared to be circular turntables — or 'round tops,' as Whittaker had somewhat ingeniously put it. Each turntable had a strong metal ring in the center to which was attached a chain. Each chain went to a separate winch that held the chain taut.

'Top of the imitation pillars of course,' Garth said. 'What about 'em?'

'I'm wondering why they need chains on. Are they movable, or something?'

'Soon find out — '

94

They went across to the nearest one and Whittaker experimentally turned the winch handle. Immediately the turntable began to rise gently, and below it there came in view part of the top of the granite pillar from below.

'Take it easy,' Garth said abruptly. 'You may bring the whole damned pillar down, or something. Obvious what the idea is: The pillars are imitation and purely ornamental. They can be raised or lowered, probably for cleaning or something. Let's get back to those spotlights.'

Whittaker nodded, returned the turntable to its normal socket, then with a thoughtful face followed Garth down through the trap and back to the spotlight platform. By this time it had cooled sufficiently for Garth to handle it — but even so, when he had opened the back, there was nothing abnormal to be seen about the set-up. Certainly the lamp, rating 1,000-watts, was of a high order for a spotlamp, but beyond this somewhat unusual point there was nothing suspicious. Except —

'These slots here,' Garth said, indicating them lying between the lamp socket and the condenser lens. 'Shouldn't something be here? They travel to the exterior of the lamphouse and look as though they should have something fitted in them.'

'Yes, sir — gelatine filters,' Whittaker responded. 'To give varying colors. The accepted thing on a modern lamp of this type.'

'Mmmm so that's it. I don't know much about spotlamps . . . Well!' Garth closed the lamp up again. 'Not getting very far, are we?'

Whittaker's eyes gave a gloomy assent, then because it was more than obvious that there was not much else to be done he led the way down to the stage again. At distance enough to be out of earshot of the constable he made a solemn pronouncement.

'Since we seem to be out of our depth on both the disappearance of Vera and the cause of Crafto's murder I'm wondering, sir, if we oughtn't to call in outside help.'

'If you're thinking about Dr. Carruthers, forget it! I refuse to have that scientific cocksure know-all mixed up with our problems if there's any way to circumvent it.'

Whittaker did not comment even though he had the instinctive feeling that, sooner or later, Hiram Carruthers would have to be consulted. He could understand Garth's reluctance well enough for the brilliant little physicist-investigator — ex back-room expert of the war department — was quite the most insufferable egotist ever. But he *did* know his job when it came to a really tough problems

'No, we'll try every avenue first,' Garth decided. 'I said last night that first thing this morning you should look into the records and see if there's anything on tap concerning Vera Kestrel or Sidney Laycock. The moment we get back lose yourself in C.R.O. until you find something.'

'Very well, sir. And you? Have you any particular move in mind?'

'For the moment,' Garth said slowly,

'I'm going to push the murder of Crafto out of my sight and instead concentrate on the Vera disappearance. Since I can't deal with two things simultaneously I'll take the problems in their correct order. I'm going to make a search of Vera's personal effects. Armed with a warrant to do that I might be lucky in finding some clue.'

Whittaker looked somewhat dubious. 'I'm not too hopeful, sir.'

'Well I *am*. Here's why — Vera must, at some time, have had some communication with somebody which might throw light on either that past mysterious financial incident of which she spoke, or else upon the events leading up to her disappearance. There might even be a diary. Lots of young women keep one, particularly if they're up to something unusual or romantic. Anyway, it's worth a try. Once I can get the vaguest clue I can really start to do something.'

So it was decided and the return to the Yard was made. Once here, Whittaker took himself to the Criminal Records Office, not with any high hope of success, and Garth secured the necessary search warrant for the examination of Vera's effects. With this as his authority there was nothing to stop him making a detailed examination of the sumptuous bedroom used by the girl before her puzzling disappearance.

The various clothes and feminine dig-dags did not interest Garth in the least: there was nothing to be gained here. Most of his attention was concentrated on the small antique bureau beside the window, the locked drawers of which he unfastened with a master-key.

There was no actual diary, but in one of the drawers there lay a considerable number of letters, some thrust back into their torn envelopes, and most of them in that superb state of untidiness common to a young and mainly irresponsible woman.

It struck Garth as odd, as he sat at the bureau and glanced through the letters, that not one of them was from Sidney Laycock. Keeping the engagement in mind he would have thought that there would have been several romantic exchanges — which he would have skimmed over in any case — but there was no such thing. Either Sidney Laycock was too worldly wise to express his emotions in black and white, which might be used against him later; or else Vera had destroyed them upon receipt . . . No, of communication between Laycock and Vera there was no trace, but there *were* quite a few letters from one Robert Alroyd, and the surprising thing was that here there *was* a definite element of romance, and extended towards Vera too.

Scowling, Garth read one of the letters through carefully:

Desmond Chambers,
Ansell Street, W.C.2

My dear Vera,

Thinking it over, maybe the proposition you put forward last night isn't so outlandish after all. The only thing I have against it is that it does not go far enough: however, maybe I can rectify that for myself. You, dear creature, do not seem to realize that in involving a third party there is a certain element of risk. However, we can talk this over together later. Meantime, remember that you mean more to me than anything else in the world and I'll do everything I can to make a success of this startling idea of yours. Until we next meet.

Ever Yours,
BOB.

'Mmmm,' Garth grunted, and picked up the further letters from the evidently amorous 'Bob'. In each case they were headed 'Desmond Chambers, Ansell Street, W.C.2,' but it was from a visiting card that Garth discovered the full name to be Robert Alroyd, and his occupation was delineated as 'Patentees' Agent.' The letters in themselves contained nothing significant and were mainly romantic rot, as far as Garth was concernd. He was not the kind of man to be moved by statements likening Vera's eyes to the stars over the western desert at twilight.

'Proposition — startling idea,' he muttered, stacking the letters together and putting them in his brief-case. 'May be something in that. Pity I've no replies as Vera sent them — but then, she'd hardly take a carbon copy of her romantic moments. Now, what else have we . . . ?'

Precious little apparently — until he came to her bank pass-book, that most telltale of all books when it comes to assessing the owner's affairs. Carefully, Garth went through it. In the main, of course, the items made little sense, but his eyes did widen slightly at the immense amount of money possessed by this mysterious young woman who had vanished from human ken. One entry in particular held his attention by the size of the amount. It was a debit of £250,000 — which hardly made any difference to her total account! — made payable to Leslie Gantry. Who Leslie Gantry might be was anybody's guess.

'Bank might know,' Garth mused. 'Might see if they'll open up for a change . . . '

In this, though, he was unlucky. Vera's bank manager refused to divulge a single thing, and as Garth knew this was well within the manager's rights since Vera, though she had mysteriously vanished, had not been proven dead. Until this happened her bank had the right to withhold, even from Scotland Yard, as much information as it chose. So Garth was forced to continue on his way bitterly reflecting on the anomaly of legislation that prevents banks working hand-in-glove with law and order.

Very flatulent and dispirited Garth arrived back at his office overlooking the Thames Embankment towards lunch-time. He found Whittaker already present, a look of suppressed eagerness on his usually inscrutable face.

'I had a bit of luck in Crow, sir,' he announced, using the technical slang for Criminal Records Office. 'I've found a case dating back seven years, concerning murder. It was in the 'Cases Uncompleted' section, so evidently it was never brought to a successful conclusion. The main person in it was this one . . . '

Whittaker handed over a carefully itemized card to which was attached the usual full face and profile of the person concerned. Garth gave a start as he studied the photograph.

'Damn me, that's Vera Kestrel!'

'I think so too, Sir. Good deal younger, and her hair dark, but otherwise there isn't much doubt.'

Definitely it *was* Vera. She had a kind of donkey-fringe hair-do and looked around eighteen, which was compatible with her present age.

'You've seen her in the flesh,' Garth remarked, 'whereas I have only had that cabinet photograph. What's your view?'

'I'd stake everything I've got, sir, that it's Vera. And read what she was mixed up in . . .'

Garth did so, wading through the mass of detail to the main point — which was that the girl, here named as Ethel Martin, was to be kept under observation in connection with the murder of one Michael Ayrton, of Kimberley Mansions, London. From this there stemmed a report of the case as given by the Chief-Inspector then in charge, ending with the regretful conclusion that there was not enough evidence to prefer a charge against the 'aforesaid Ethel Martin.'

'Well, if it isn't Vera Kestrel I'm a Chinaman,' Garth declared. 'Pity is that no fingerprints are given — impossible, of course, until conviction. We could easily have got some left by Vera and checked them against this. The law certainly doesn't help us sometimes, m'lad.'

'No, sir,' Whittaker admitted. 'However, I think we can take it that this girl in the photograph is also Vera. That *could* tie up with that doubtful incident in the past that she mentioned. Only she said it was *financial* — or at least that was what I understood.'

Garth thumped his chest and rifted noisily as he thought the matter out.

'Financial, eh?' he muttered at length. 'Tied up with some incident in the past. And didn't that link up again with some remark about her fiancé, Laycock?'

'That's right, sir. All three, as I gathered, were the main reason for her needing police protection at the magical demonstration, strange though it may seem.'

'Mmmm ... I'm going to hazard a guess. Vera, at one time, under the alias of

Ethel Martin, was mixed up with the murder of Michael Ayrton. She couldn't be charged because of lack of evidence. Right so far . . . Now, Sidney Laycock might possibly have known something about that business and therefore had a hold over Vera. That would account for their utter disregard for each other's feelings despite the fact that they are to be married. Maybe Vera has — or had — to marry Laycock to keep his mouth shut. It might be his price to keep quiet about her. Offhand, he seems just the kind of swine who *would* pursue a deal of that sort.'

'Nice theory, sir, anyway,' Whittaker admitted.

'I can't fit in the obvious possibility of blackmail by Laycock,' Garth continued, 'because according to Vera's pass-book, which I've carefully examined, there are no signs of any payments to Laycock.'

Whittaker smiled. 'That's no criterion, sir. She could have paid out the sums to an alias, or even drawn it on 'Self' and paid in cash.'

'You're very bright this morning.'

Garth growled. 'But, by jimmy, you're right enough. I admit those possibilities, but I have to work on what is before me. Okay for the moment: we've made slight headway. After lunch get every detail of this Ayrton case from the records and let me have them. I've a call to make — on one Robert Alroyd.'

'Oh?' Whittaker frowned. 'Where does *he* fit in, sir? I don't recall the name.'

'For your information he's Vera's real lover — as apart from fiancé, or at least. I think so. I got it all from Vera's personal letters this morning . . . We're moving, my boy, though I'm damned if I know at the moment in which direction.'

Upon which note Garth shut down on everything for the time being and retired for lunch with the hunger of a dyspeptic. The moment he had finished it he drove himself out to Desmond Chambers, in Ansell Street, and here met his first setback. Amongst all the nameplates, one was missing — and apparently it was the one that had belonged to Robert Alroyd.

Chewing his cheroot in annoyance Garth went in search of the caretaker and finally located him. This gnarled individual's reluctance to be civil was quickly cured as he saw the warrant-card in Garth's hand.

'I'm looking for Mr. Alroyd.' Garth explained. 'Apparently he's moved from here.'

'That's right, Inspector.'

'When?'

'Be about two weeks ago, far as I can remember.'

'But surely he left a forwarding address?' Garth demanded.

'Not as I know of, sir. I did 'ear some talk about 'im going abroad, but I don't know *whereabouts* abroad.'

'I see . . .' Garth inhaled deeply at his cheroot and mused. Then, 'He was a Patentees' agent, wasn't he? What sort of a business was that?'

'Far as I know, sir, 'e 'andled the works of inventors and such like. Got them in with the Patent Offices, or something, and charged a fee for doin' it.'

'Uh-huh; now I understand. All right, many thanks.'

And not much wiser Garth returned to

Scotland Yard, becoming gradually more bad-tempered as his lunch refused to digest. He threw himself down at his desk and pondered, a fresh cheroot smouldering at the corner of his merciless mouth. After a while he began to make notes:

1. Vera Kestrel vanishes.
2. Vera Kestrel and Ethel Martin probably same person. Latter involved in possible murder.
3. Vera and Sidney Laycock engaged, and always at loggerheads with each other.
4. Crafto, involved in the vanishment, is murdered. Possible method — Poison gas.
5. Sidney Laycock is a *chemist*.
6. Vera's possible real lover is Robert Alroyd who vanished to somewhere abroad two weeks ago.

Possibility 1:
Did Vera go with him, which explains why she has so completely disappeared?
Possibility 2:
Did Crafto know every detail of the

disappearance, despite his superb acting to the contrary, and was murdered in case he talked too much?
Possibility 3:
That Laycock, a chemist, murdered Crafto.

Unsolved: Vera's disappearance from the cage.
Unsolved: The method of killing Crafto.

Individual Points:

1. Bar five on the cage is unique.
2. The limelights are unnecessarily powerful and hot.

Garth sighed, massaging the bulges on his jaw. Then he glanced up as Whittaker came in, a sheaf of papers in his hand. He had that composedly complacent smile which suggested he had discovered something interesting.

'All yours, sir,' he said, putting the papers down on the desk.

Garth was not listening. He was staring

straight before him, distance in his keen eyes.

' 'You, dear creature, do not seem to realize that in involving a third party there is a certain element of risk. I will do everything *I* can to make a success of this startling idea of yours . . . ' A *third* party, Whitty! That may be something.'

'Yes, sir.' Whittaker tried to look interested. 'Might I have the facts, sir?'

'Take too long. I was just repeating the words written by Robert Alroyd to Vera Kestrel. Somehow, we've got to find this man Alroyd. He may even be Leslie Gantry, to whom she paid two hundred and fifty thousand pounds. Or, equally, Gantry could be Laycock receiving hush money.'

Whittaker sighed. 'I'm afraid I'm way behind you now, sir. Sorry.'

Garth grinned round his cheroot. 'Vera paid that sum recently to somebody named Gantry, and the bank won't open up and say where he's to be found. The other information was in a letter from Bob — Robert — Alroyd to Vera, and she had evidently put an unusual proposition

111

to him. It is possible that this fellow Alroyd might have been mixed up in the murder of Crafto. So could Laycock, since he's a chemist, and therefore used to dealing in poisons.'

'And what occupation has Alroyd?' Whittaker questioned.

'He was a Patentee's agent — arranged deals between the Patent Offices and inventors. I have heard of such beings, but they're rare.'

'Which puts guilt equally on Alroyd's shoulders as far as professional skill is concerned,' Whittaker said. 'A Patentees' agent has access to all plans and specifications. He's the man who can study everybody's inventions. He might, in a modified form, use any of them to his own advantage.'

'What's that got to do with it?' Garth asked bluntly.

'I don't know, sir — unless one of these inventions gave him an idea to make Vera vanish.'

Garth gave a start. 'By jimmy, I never thought of that angle! Go to the top of the class, m'lad.'

Whittaker smiled modestly. 'Only a thought, sir, and maybe dead wrong — but I agree with you that Alroyd aught to be located.'

'That's the tough part: he's gone abroad. Only thing we can do is ask the air line companies and shipping authorities to check their lists for two weeks back and see if they have Alroyd listed.'

'I'll do that immediately, sir,' Whittaker said, and turned to the 'phone whilst Garth picked up the papers on the Michael Ayrton case which had been laid before him. The details, thorough though they were, did not in essence tell him much more than he had gleaned already — namely that Michael Ayrton had been shot in his flat by a person or persons unknown one summer's evening in June, and the woman Ethel Martin had been seen leaving his apartment. The flaws in the evidence were obvious and to the trained eye of Garth it was obvious why the case had fallen to bits, but of one thing he was certain: Vera Kestrel and Ethel Martin were the same person. Doubtless, whatever scandal there might have been had been hushed up by her father's immense influence. There was no doubt of one thing: other people could have been involved in the affair of Michael Ayrton, and Sidney Laycock — or even Robert Alroyd — could have been two of them.

'Nothing, sir,' Whittaker said, and Garth looked at him absently.

'Nothing? What the blazes are you talking about?'

'I mean Robert Alroyd isn't mentioned in the passenger lists of the last fortnight, either by sea or air. I've just checked on it. He must have changed his name.'

'And nobody changes his or her name without a guilty reason,' Garth muttered. 'All right, we'll have to use other methods. Get me Kestrel: he may even know of this blighter and what he looks like.'

But here Garth ran up a blind alley, or else the industrialist was lying.

'Never heard of him,' came Kestrel's heavy voice. 'Are you sure of your facts? Vera is — or was — engaged to Sidney Laycock. I thought you knew that.'

'I do know it, but her heart was obviously given to another. I'm taking a shot in the dark — that she may have gone away with him and that he helped to engineer her disappearance.'

'Damned rubbish!' Kestrel decided bluntly. 'And what right had you to go poking around amongst my daughter's effects? That surely wasn't necessary?'

'It was *very* necessary. All lines of enquiry are so blocked I had to launch out. This Robert Alroyd definitely appears to exist and I'm surprised your daughter never mentioned him.'

'She hardly would if she wanted to keep him a secret, would she?' Kestrel's tone changed abruptly. 'Look, Inspector, my daughter's disappearance still remains as big a mystery as ever and all you seem to do is get deeper in the mire. And there's Crafto's murder added to it — and the inquest on him tomorrow afternoon, to which I have to go. Stop playing around and get some action. If you don't I'll say a few things to the Assistant Commissioner. Don't forget, he's a personal friend.'

The line clicked and Garth bit so hard on his cheroot he broke off the end. Savagely he banged the stub in the ash-tray

'Hear that?' he demanded, with a bleak glance at Whittaker.

'I did, sir, yes.

'Who the devil does he think he is, I wonder? Treating me like some no-account boy scout'

'I'm afraid he's one of the most powerful men in the country and he *can* be very nasty if he chooses.'

'Damn him!' Garth swore. 'We're doing our best, aren't we?'

'No doubt of it — but Kestrel is a man of action and his daughter is as far away as ever. Can't blame him for getting edgy. We're all tangled up with no clear lead to follow.'

Garth brooded as he popped a magnesia tablet in his mouth, then he looked up as an officer came in.

'This has just arrived for you, sir. Must have been delivered by hand in the main letter box . . . '

'Okay, thanks.' Garth took the envelope

and eyed it without much interest. The writing was sprawling and in dead black ink. The superscription read:

Inspector Garth, C.I.D.,
Scotland Yard.

'Now what?' Garth growled, tearing the flap; then when he read the sprawled, backwardly tilted writing he sat up in his chair, a look of such fixed intentness in his eyes that Whittaker too caught something of his interest. At the end of the letter Garth stared in front of him and then jerked his head.

'Read this over my shoulder, Whitty. See what you make of it.'

Whittaker obeyed, becoming more surprised as his eyes covered each line:

Inspector Garth,
Scotland Yard.

Dear Sir,

I've seen in the papers that you're working on the mystery of Vera Kestrel's disappearance. I've also seen her photo in the paper. It says in the papers that other people at the magic show was Sidney Laycock and some other people. Which brings me to what I've seen. I don't want my name to be known because I don't want to be pestered with questions — but this I'll tell you. I'm usually against the cops because I'm a cat burglar.

Last night I climbed into a small laboratory in Pine Street, near Marble Arch, because I thought it would be an easy way to reach a house near it at the back. In that laboratory I saw a big empty bath and I'll stake my soul there was acid stains in it. But I also saw a girl's clothes hanging on a door, and there was an evening-gown which looks like the one described as being worn by Miss Kestrel when she vanished. What makes all this important is that this place I got into belongs to Sidney Laycock. I found that out when I left by the door. His nameplate is outside. I don't like murder, and it looks as if this might be that, so I thought I'd risk telling you.

Informer.

'Well?' Garth asked, who relied on Whittaker's stolid opinions far more than he admitted.

'Seems genuine,' Whittaker said finally. 'Very often the 'higher' type of crook turns informer on murder, and this looks like one of those cases. Certainly Laycock himself would hardly draw attention to a thing like this and, offhand, I can't think of anybody else who would. Maybe we'd better go and look.'

'No maybe about it,' Garth retorted, jumping up. 'On our way . . .'

And a patrol car did the rest, finishing its journey in one of London's queerer back streets where, sandwiched between two big houses of the Georgian variety, there stood a fairly modern low-roofed building with a large sign over the single door. It read:

SIDNEY LAYCOCK
CHEMICAL ENTERPRISES LABORATORY

'No doubt about that,' Garth said. 'And presumably our cat burglar friend was aiming at one of the houses on either side. We can't go busting in here without authority — which we haven't got. You'd better ring Laycock, Whitty, and have him come over immediately with the key. There's a kiosk at the corner.'

Whittaker obeyed and climbed out of the car, returning in a few minutes with the information that Laycock would do as requested — but with reluctance, since his business demanded his whole attention.

'So does this,' Garth growled. 'Only thing I'm afraid of is that he may have removed the evidences we're hoping to find.'

'I don't understand,' Whittaker mused, 'why he has left them lying around at all. Damned thoughtless of him, unless he felt thoroughly safe.'

Garth rumbled internally but passed no comment. He lighted a cheroot and was half-way through it when at last Laycock's car appeared, drawing up a yard or two away. His sensual face was looking disagreeably surprised as he saw Garth and Whittaker awaiting him.

'Am I entitled to ask the reason for

this, Inspector, or is it a top secret?'

'Purely routine enquiry.' Garth replied briefly. 'I warned you that I'd probably be in touch with you again. Open up, if you please.'

Laycock shrugged and did as he was bidden, afterwards leading the way down a short stone corridor to a solitary door. Opening this again with a Yale key he switched on the lights, which immediately mitigated the gloom cast by the buildings rearing up against the frosted glass windows.

Then, in walking casually across the fairly big laboratory, Laycock came to a sudden stop. Garth and Whittaker stopped too as they saw that Laycock's eyes were fixed on a collection of feminine garments, together with a cocktail gown, hanging on a hook on the nearby wall.

5

'Now you know why we're here, Mr. Laycock.' Garth said grimly, and at that Laycock swung and stared at him.

'What kind of a game is this?' he demanded. 'Who the hell planted those clothes there?'

'That's rather a silly question, isn't it?' Garth asked, and moved forward to gaze at the clothes more intently. He took good care not to touch them, however, and promptly restrained Laycock as he was about to do so.

'Take a look around, Whitty,' Garth ordered. 'I've a few things to ask Mr. Laycock.'

Whittaker began to move, first in the direction of the empty bath that had been mentioned in the cat burglar's letter. Laycock stood in silence, his expression a mixture of fury and alarm. Deep down, though, Garth suspected, he was far more puzzled than furious

— unless he was a good actor.

'You recognize these clothes?' Garth asked curtly.

'I recognize the cocktail gown, certainly: it's the one Vera wore at the magical demonstration. Presumably the rest of the finery is hers, too.'

'So I think. How did they get here?'

'You can please yourself whether you believe it or not, but I just don't know.'

'You can do better than that, Mr. Laycock!'

'I don't *know*, I tell you! It's as big a surprise to me as to anybody that they should be here.'

Garth glanced dourly about him, then back to the chemist.

'When were you last here?'

'About a week ago. I don't come very often, only when there is some especial job to be done. This place is a subsidiary to my shop.'

'I gathered that. Have you a 'phone here?'

Laycock nodded towards the nearby bench and Garth crossed to the instrument and raised it. In a few moments he was through to Scotland Yard.

'Garth here. Send down a fingerprint man and photographer to Laycock Chemical Enterprises in Pine Street, Marble Arch.'

This done Garth reflected for a moment and then turned as Whittaker came towards him.

'Better take a look at that bath, sir. See what you think of it.'

Garth moved to it. The bath was made of nickel steel and was evidently intended for use with acid. Even so the nickel steel was not so perfect that it was unblemished. There was a distinct acid tide-mark all the way round it — and in the base of the bath something was gleaming brightly. His eyes sharp, Garth peered at it, then with his pocket forceps he picked the object up gently and studied it under the nearest electric light.

'Gold,' he murmured, as Whittaker gazed with him. 'A gold shell. Sort of thing you get on a tooth sometimes.'

'My God!' Whittaker muttered. 'This business has taken a sudden dive into the macabre, sir. Vera Kestrel had a gold tooth, or else a tooth with a gold cap. I remember noticing it.'

Laycock, who had been standing listening to the low-toned conversation, came forward suddenly. Perhaps it was rather surprising that he made no effort to dash for it, for the doors were wide open.

'What are you two trying to pin on me?' he demanded, and Garth gave him a sharp look.

'It's not my job to try and pin anything, Laycock, and well you know it. I'm working by inference . . . In this bath, in which there has obviously been a powerful corrosive acid, we find a gold shell from a tooth. Gold is resistant to acid, as you must know as a chemist, and it hasn't dissolved with whatever else was in this bath. On the wall are the clothes belonging to Vera Kestrel — at any rate the cocktail gown and doubtless the other fal-de-lals can be identified later. You'll save yourself a lot of trouble if you'll give a straight answer.'

'I've no answer to give. This whole

business is faked: I swear it is! I haven't even been here in the past week.'

Garth looked about him and finally towards the nearby carboys which, in their wicker stands, were variously labeled — 'Pure Sulphuric'; 'Nitric'; 'Hydrochloric'. There were three labeled 'Nitric,' but two of them were empty.

'What happened to those empty carboys?' Garth demanded, and Laycock gave a bewildered shake of his head.

'I don't know. They were full when I was last here.'

Garth stopped talking. He dropped the gold tooth-cap into the cellophane envelope that Whittaker held out to him, then he went on a slow prowl around the remainder of the laboratory. Several sharp cutting knives and a small hacksaw engaged his attention, even though they appeared spotlessly clean. Handling them still with his forceps he manoeuvred them into the bigger cellophane bag that Whittaker provided for him then he turned back to Laycock.

'So you've nothing to say, Mr. Laycock?'

'I can't tell you what I don't *know*, can I?'

'Who else knows of this laboratory of yours?'

'Quite a few people. Several members of my shop staff, and Vera of course. Mr. Kestrel, too.'

'Anybody by the name of Robert Alroyd know of it?'

Laycock shook his head. 'Never heard of him.' Then in sudden desperation he went on: 'Look here, Inspector, see this thing in its proper perspective! You're suggesting, but not in so many words, that I've had Vera here and done away with her in a bath of acid. You *then* suggest that I, as a professional chemist, and up to all the dodges, would overlook that she had a gold tooth that would resist the acid. After that I'm supposed to be chump enough to leave all Vera's clothes hanging on a peg for everybody to see, and not even take the trouble to properly clean out the acid bath afterwards.'

'You could have been in too much of a hurry to clean it, and thereby missed seeing the gold tooth lying at the bottom.

You could have left the acid to empty itself out and then have hurried away.'

'Leaving those clothes there as direct evidence? I call that an insult to my intelligence!'

Whatever Garth was going to say was interrupted by the arrival of the finger-print men and photographers. Their task took them twenty minutes, and when they left they also took with them the objects in the cellophane envelopes for closer investigation, and the missing Vera's clothes for study by the pathological section. This done Garth turned back to Laycock.

'I'll thank you for the key to this place, Mr. Laycock.'

The chemist handed it over slowly, frowning. 'And what happens to me? I suppose you're going to arrest me?'

'On what charge?'

'You've made it pretty plain that you think I murdered Vera!'

'Maybe I have, but I'm a policeman, Mr. Laycock, and without a corpus delicti I can't do a thing. For the moment, until there is reasonable proof for a conviction,

128

you're as you were — but I'm still warning you not to leave town without permission.'

'I won't.' Obvious relief spread over Laycock's heavy face. 'Tell me something: what in the world put you onto this line of enquiry?'

'Never mind — Oh, there's one other thing,' Garth added, as Laycock turned to the doorway. 'Did you ever hear of a man by the name of Michael Ayrton?'

For an instant Sidney Laycock was caught out. He gave a distinct start and a momentary look of consternation crossed his face. It was all extremely brief, but it did not escape either Garth or Whittaker.

'No,' Laycock said, 'I never heard of him . . . '

Then probably so he could not be questioned further he left the laboratory.

'Liar,' Garth commented, with a hard grin. 'I have more than a feeling, Whitty, that Sidney Laycock may be one of the unmentioned witnesses to the uncompleted Michael Ayrton case. However, we'll let that ride for the moment.'

'Yes, sir,' Whittaker assented, and then

he changed the subject quickly, 'I get the impression, sir, that our cat burglar friend was a remarkably skilled man in order to get into and out of here. He hasn't left a trace. Not so much as a whisker. I made sure of that whilst I was prowling around. We can take it as certain that he didn't have a duplicate key to the door, which means he could only have used one or other of these windows. Take a look at them. They only open at the top and I never saw catches less disturbed.'

Garth clambered up and looked, only to satisfy himself that Whittaker's observation was entirely correct.

'The other thing is,' Whittaker continued, 'why did he find it necessary, I wonder, to come through here in order to reach one or other of the houses to either side? They're completely detached, so I can't see the object.'

'There are a lot of things about this business where the object can't be seen,' Garth commented. ''Phone for a man to be sent down here to keep watch whilst we get back to the Yard. I want to hear

130

what sort of a report the pathological department has to offer.'

Whittaker did as instructed and the moment the constable had arrived to do duty the return to the Yard was made. Even so, Garth had to be content with the news that pathology was not yet ready to make its report.

'More time wasted!' Garth growled, sorting out his various notes preparatory to giving them careful study.

'We do all the hard work and they do all the slacking.' He reached out to the intercom as it buzzed sharply. 'Yes? Garth here.'

'Oh, you're back, Mortimer.' It was the voice of the Assistant Commissioner. 'Would you come along and have a word with me.'

'Right away, sir,' Garth assented, and grimaced as he switched off and met the eyes of Whittaker.

'He didn't sound in too good a temper, sir,' Whittaker commented.

'He never does.' Garth straightened his tie, tidied his wiry hair as well as possible, and then left the office.

When he reached the Assistant Commissioner's domain he found the situation pretty much as he had expected to find it. Besides the A.C. himself — boss of the C.I.D. Metropolitan Division — there was also the stolid, perfectly tailored figure of Victor de Maine-Kestrel. And neither man was looking particularly cordial.

'Have a seat, Mortimer,' the A.C. invited. 'Just a few things want straightening out. You know Mr. de Maine — Kestrel?

'I've had the pleasure,' Garth assented, settling down.

'Quite rightly, his anxiety concerning the continued disappearance of his daughter is causing him a lot of mental stress, and that in turn is affecting his business acumen.'

'I'm sorry to hear it,' Garth growled.

'Just being sorry isn't enough for me, Inspector,' Kestrel said curtly. 'You've been playing around with this problem for quite a bit of time and beyond asking questions — and not getting particularly helpful answers — you don't seem to have got anywhere. Dammit, you must have *some* kind of lead by now surely? Some suggestion to offer concerning Vera's disappearance?'

'Not yet,' Garth replied stolidly. 'When I have you'll be the first to know.'

'Just how far have you got?' the A.C. asked. His tone was neither hostile nor cordial: it was perfectly clear he was trying to placate Garth and stay on the right side of the powerful industrialist as well.

'Matter of fact, sir, in the course of my wide experience I have rarely come up against a case with so many angles. The time involved in following each one to its logical source is considerable.'

'What angles, for instance?' Kestrel demanded, and as Garth hesitated, the A.C. gave a nod.

'You can speak before Mr. Kestrel, Mortimer. It makes no difference.'

'Very well, sir. The order of the problems lies like this — One: Vera vanishes. Two: Crafto, instrumental in her disappearance, is found murdered, probably gassed, by means and person as yet

133

undiscovered. The inquest upon him will be tomorrow afternoon. Three: The cage from which Vera vanished presents certain interesting features that I haven't had time to look into yet, and the same can be said of the false roof of the theatre-ballroom in your home, Mr. Kestrel. Four: Vera, some four years ago, under the name of Ethel Martin was involved in a murder scandal concerning one Michael Ayrton — '

'That's a damned lie!' Kestrel exploded, his face coloring.

'I'm only stating facts, sir.' Garth gave him a phlegmatic glance. 'Five: Mixed up in that Michael Ayrton affair there was, I think, Sidney Laycock, Vera's fiancé. Six: Vera paid the handsome sum of two hundred and fifty thousand pounds recently to somebody named Leslie Gantry. Seven: She had a lover, a real one I think, named Robert Alroyd, who has now gone abroad. Eight: Laycock has a subsidiary laboratory to his chemical firm in which have been found Vera's clothes — everything she wore on the night of her disappearance, and right now the pathological department is investigating them. In that lab was Vera's gold tooth, lying at the bottom of a stainless bath which had recently contained nitric acid! That's the lot, and you say I'm not getting anywhere! Dammit. Mr. Kestrel, I hardly know which to tackle *first*!'

Kestrel had a fixed look of horror on his bulldog face.

'Did — did you say an *acid* bath, Inspector?'

'I did. And your daughter's clothes on a hook.'

'And the laboratory belongs to Sidney Laycock? You've arrested him, of course?'

'Not yet. I have no evidence.'

'No *evidence*!'

'In that the Inspector is right, Mr. Kestrel,' the A.C. explained. 'Nobody can be charged with any particular crime until all the facts check up. What does Laycock say about it, Mortimer?'

'Denies the whole thing.'

'Naturally he will!' Kestrel snapped. 'And look here — I don't give a damn for your evidence or the need to get proof. I demand that Laycock be charged with murder. An acid bath, my daughter's clothes, and now it seems Laycock was involved in some kind of murder business in the past. The whole thing's as plain as day.'

'Not to me, sir,' Garth said, unmoved. 'And I have to follow the letter of the law. So have you, even if you are one of the most powerful men in the country.'

Kestrel breathed hard but he kept his emotions under control.

'Yes, I have the law to obey. I suppose — but for God's sake man, get things moving. Either find out what happened to my daughter, arrest somebody for her murder, or *something*!'

'I will at the earliest moment, Mr. Kestrel. I don't like a case dragging on any more than you do.'

Kestrel hesitated and then got to his feet. 'Very well, I shall have to leave it at that. I shall be all anxiety until I hear from you again.'

With that he shook hands and departed. Garth gave the A.C. a grim glance across the desk.

'I'm doing the best I can, sir,' he said

defensively. 'I'm not a magician, you know.'

'I'm aware of it, Mortimer, and I've every faith in you — but I *do* think you're perhaps tackling too much at once. Tell me, how do you think Vera disappeared from that cage thing?'

'I don't know. The cage has me beaten.'

'Then how do you propose to solve it?'

Garth pinched finger and thumb in his eyes. 'Matter of fact I was leaving that bit until last. It isn't the problem itself: it is only an offshoot thereof. I've been trying to find out what happened to Vera because that's the main point. The next main point is the death of Crafto and how it was caused . . . '

'Any suspicions?'

'Plenty. I think he was killed by some scientific means or other; just as I think Vera's disappearance was engineered by a scientific method.'

'Then you'll have to delegate that part of the case to a specialist in such matters. I mean Dr. Carruthers, of course.'

'I was afraid you did, sir,' Garth sighed.

'I know you don't like him, but that's

beside the point. He knows his job and we must have some action. Kestrel is one of the few men who can use his influence to bring the Yard into bad odor if he wants, and that won't do. See Carruthers and ask him to take on the scientific side, whilst you follow up the other leads — this Robert Alroyd, for one, and Leslie Gantry for another. You've no ideas about Leslie Gantry, I suppose?'

'At the moment the only one I can think of is that he might be a scientist to whom Vera paid a vast sum to engineer her mystical disappearance. Gantry perhaps arranged her queer vanishing act and smuggled her to heaven knows where. Afterwards, again using his scientific streak, he killed Crafto somehow because he knew too much. If that sounds too much like a cheap thriller I can't help it. It's the way it looks anyhow.'

'And Vera Kestrel? You really think she was murdered and her remains disposed of in an acid bath by Sidney Laycock?'

Garth shook his head. 'No, I don't. That's one reason why I made no attempt to arrest Laycock. To my mind the whole thing is too infernally obvious — too studied, too planted. On top of that I really believe that Laycock was as astounded as anybody to discover so many evidences of Vera lying around. On the other hand he obviously wouldn't plant all that evidence himself in case he got landed for murder. So my suspicions switch back to either Leslie Gantry or Robert Alroyd, probably the latter. Though how on earth he gained access to the laboratory I don't know . . . Or maybe I do. Vera was Laycock's fiancée and she must have known of the existence of this separate laboratory. She could probably have found a way to get the key to it, or a wax impression thereof . . . '

Garth stopped and sighed. 'The whole thing's one hell of a Chinese puzzle, sir.'

'I agree with you, and I know the legal limitations under which you have to work. Carry straight on and get Carruthers to do the specialized work. In the meantime I'll keep Kestrel as mollified as possible.'

'Okay, sir.' Garth got to his feet and then paused as he saw that the A.C. was hesitating over something.

'I suppose . . . ' The A.C. looked up. 'I suppose you haven't got Kestrel himself on your list of suspects?'

'I'm afraid I have, yes. One is as guilty as another to me until I've done the weeding out.'

Twinging with indigestion Garth left the office and returned in a bleak mood to his own quarters. By this time the pathological reports had come in and Whittaker was in the midst of studying them. He glanced up quickly as his boss came in.

'Anything serious, sir?' he asked anxiously.

'Only a metaphorical kick on the behind and orders to get Beethoven do the scientific work.'

Whittaker sighed. 'I knew it would come to that sooner or later. Maybe as well, too, for from the look of this report we have more nasty work on our hands. The various instruments and the hacksaw you took from the lab have traces of human tissue and dried blood on them. Group O. There's a bloodstain on Vera's cocktail gown, of the same group. They both aglutinize to the same test, so it begins to look as though she got the works . . . Take a look for yourself, sir.'

Garth picked up the reports and read them carefully. Divested of their technical trimmings they inferred quite plainly that the traces of tissue, mainly discovered between the teeth of the hacksaw — despite obvious efforts to clean it — were human, and that the bloodstains, microscopic though they were and which had been left behind on the knife blade, were human blood of the O group. Identical group stains were on the cocktail gown . . . As far as fingerprints were concerned there were two sets constantly repeated. One apparently belonged to Sidney Laycock, since they were on many of the jars of the laboratory also, and the other set, feminine, could belong to Vera Kestrel. Without something personal of her own, known to have been handled by her, this was impossible to check. They were mostly prevalent upon the sides of the acid bath and on the hilt of one of the knives.

'Pretty conclusive, eh, sir?' Whittaker

asked, and received, quite a surprise at the answer.

'Like hell it is, my lad! When that girl was put in the bath — if she was put in the bath — she would either be dead or else alive and tightly bound. Her killer certainly wouldn't take the chance of leaving her with her arms and hands free whereby she might lash out at him. Why, then, the prints on the bath sides, and *clear* ones at that. The prints of a dead person are by no means clear, and if she were alive — as these clear prints seem to show — she would hardly have her hands free.'

'Quite a logical angle, sir,' Whittaker agreed. 'I hadn't thought of that.'

'The gold cap is used for covering a tooth otherwise unsightly,' Garth repeated, reading the remainder of the report.

'Which recalls something to my mind,' Whittaker said, thinking. 'I couldn't help wondering, when I was talking to Vera, why she so spoilt her otherwise pretty face with that very ostentatious gold tooth cap. It stuck out a mile, so to speak. You'd think a girl like her, careful of her appearance and darned good looking, would have had a false tooth screwed into the gum or something. Gold caps are pretty antique these days.' Garth picked up the telephone and presently was successful in contacting Victor Kestrel.

'I think you may be able to help me with a vital point, sir,' Garth explained. 'Your daughter had a gold cap on one of her upper set of teeth. You know that, of course.'

'Yes, I know it. What about it?'

'Do you know when that cap was fitted and by whom?'

'Er — let me think now.' Long pause. 'I know she'd had it put in about a month before she so tragically vanished, and the dental surgeon was a chap named — Oh, er — Sturgeon, or somebody. Quite a big noise in dentistry.'

'Would it be Adam Sturchon, the dental consultant?' Garth suggested, picking on a man whom he knew to be a top-liner.

'That's it. I can't see it matters much.'

'It may matter a lot before we're

finished, sir. Now, I'm going to send a man over for one of your daughter's hairbrushes. It's usually the most likely article for carrying fingerprints. Perhaps you'd advise them at your residence and the brush can be made ready. Tell the servant to lift the brush by the bristles and put it carefully in a paper bag.'

'All right,' the industrialist agreed. 'And tell me something else, which I didn't get around to in the Assistant Commissioner's office.'

'If I can. What is it?'

'Do you, having followed the case so far, honestly believe that my poor girl has been murdered and her remains destroyed? If so I'll hound her killer to the ends of the earth. I'll use every cent of the money I possess to — '

'I don't think that will be necessary, Mr. Kestrel. I do not think your daughter is dead — in fact, not by any means,' Garth finished ambiguously. 'And thank you for being so helpful. I'll keep in touch.'

With that he switched off and looked at Whittaker. 'On your way, Whitty, and pick up the hairbrush. We may even need the back of it later to tan Vera's posterior if what I have in mind works out. Get some tea on your way back and meet me here at seven. We'll have to do as the Chief says and have a word with Carruthers . . . confound him! Before I get my own tea I may have time to talk to Adam Sturchon.'

Whittaker nodded and went on his way. Garth reached to the telephone again and the fact that he was in the C.I.D. was enough cause for the great dental expert to answer him with the minimum of delay.

'Miss de Maine Kestrel?' the dental surgeon repeated. 'Yes, indeed, I remember attending her. I assume, Inspector, that you are at work on her astonishing disappearance?'

'I am, yes, and I think you can assist me. In your opinion, was the gold cap which Miss Kestrel had on her tooth a real necessity?'

'Do you want the answer man to man, or from a consulting dentist who attended a very wealthy and exacting young woman?'

'Man to man, please; I get on better that way.'

'Very well. There was no need whatever for the cap. The tooth it covered had been broken earlier in Miss Kestrel's life and, of course, had not grown again. Had she not possessed an inordinate fear of dentistry she could have had the half-tooth removed, and that was what I suggested. She refused and insisted instead on a gold cap. I considered the whole thing somewhat pointless since the half-tooth was not normally visible — only when she laughed extravagantly. Anyhow, she insisted, so I complied, and the gold shell was duly fitted. It didn't suit her at all, but she seemed satisfied enough.'

'And how long ago was this?'

'Oh, about a month. I can find the exact date if you — '

'No thank you, sir, that won't be necessary. Much obliged for the help.'

Garth rang off and sat musing, a grim smile on his square face.

'Light,' he murmured. 'Light in the darkness, I do believe. I could almost finish the course by myself if I could figure out the problem of the cage and the dead magician. I suppose there is nothing else for it but Carruthers . . . '

Again he lifted the telephone and gave the Halingford number of Dr. Hiram Carruthers. Halingford was thirty miles south of London, a small suburban region, and Dr. Hiram J. Carruthers, the eccentric scientist, was probably the most famous person in it.

'Speak up and make it brief,' a high-pitched voice abruptly commanded over the wire.

'Dr. Carruthers?' Garth modulated his voice to grave respect. 'Garth here.'

'What do you want, and how are you?'

'I want you, and I'm not so good. Indigestion's bad.'

'You should drink quarts of tepid tea, same as I do. And I'm busy. I've no time right now for your petty-fogging problems.'

'This isn't petty-fogging, Doc. It's the Vera Kestrel case, the girl who vanished from the silvered cage. You must have read about it, or heard of it over the television or radio.'

'Oh, that! Mmmm, I suppose it has points of interest. And Crafto's death, too. That's got you stuck in the mud too, I suppose?'

'I'm afraid it has.'

'And what's this in the early evening papers about Vera being disposed of in an acid bath in Sidney Laycock's laboratory?'

Garth reflected. 'I didn't know that had reached the Press. Maybe Laycock talked. Anyway, all three points are linked up and the A.C. says he'd be glad if you'd take time out to have a look at the scientific angle. The business is complicated more than somewhat and I can't look after everything.'

'I have doubts, Garth, if you can look after anything. All right, seven-thirty. If you're late I shan't be here. 'Bye.'

The line went dead. Muttering to himself Garth put the 'phone back on its cradle and then considered what he must take for the exacting Carruthers to inspect. Notes, of course, and that stick-pin of Crafto's with the crushed pearl, the articles from the pathological department ... Here, Garth felt, was something which was going to tax the Halingford madman to the uttermost.

Presently he had everything ready as he desired it, when his eyes fell upon the note that had been sent him by 'Informer'. He considered it for a moment, and then nodded to himself and switched on the intercom, connecting him with the calligraphic department.

'Garth here, Terry,' he explained. 'I've got a note here which needs checking. Find out all you can about it and let me know as soon as possible.'

'Okay,' assented a phlegmatic voice. 'I'll send over for it right away.'

'Thanks.' Garth switched off, and the sinister rumblings which were making themselves heard from his equator decided him that it was time he had some tea.

6

Whittaker returned to time, delivered the hairbrush to Dabs — the fingerprint department — and then he and Garth took the first available train for Halingford. It was a golden rule that Hiram Carruthers never visited Scotland Yard except by his own inclination. Enquirers, even from the Yard, had to go to *him*. If they did not, it was their hard luck.

So 7.30 found Garth and Whittaker entering that room of incredible confusion and litter, which Carruthers was pleased to call a 'study.' They found him coiled up like a gnome in the big armchair, a low fire mitigating the chill of the spring evening. In those few seconds it struck Whittaker that Carruthers had rarely looked so much like the popular busts of Beethoven, with his mane of white hair, powerful face, and jutting mouth.

As the two men were shown in by the

housekeeper he got up from the chair — a small man of cocksparrow stature standing no more than five feet — and held out his hand.

'Greetings, gentlemen. Sit down . . . There ought to be chairs somewhere . . .' Books and stacks of paper were hurled unceremoniously on the floor and eventually the two chairs came to light. Garth and Whittaker settled themselves with an air of expecting something to happen.

'Frankly,' Carruthers said, lighting a charred briar and staring at the two fixedly with his intense blue eyes, 'I wish the pair of you were at the devil! Nothing personal, but I'm deep in the middle of the Rutter case and you're nothing but an interruption.'

'Rutter case?' Garth repeated vaguely.

'Oh, don't strain yourself, man; it isn't up your alley. It concerns a north of England tea merchant who took the five-ten from Manchester and utterly disappeared en route. The Manchester police asked me to look into it . . . In fact,' the gnome continued, coiling up again in the chair, 'disappearances seem to be the fashion. Have some tea?'

Recalling the pallid muck which Carruthers drank without ceasing the two Yard men shook their heads. He shrugged, dragged out a woollen-cosied enigma from amidst the mountains of papers, and poured some of the pale yellow filth into a tannin-stained teacup.

'Well, well, go on!' he commanded. 'You've been here five-and-a-half minutes and done nothing but look at me. What's it all about? And if you say Vera Kestrel I'll crown you because I know that already!'

Garth cleared his throat, strangled a belch, and sailed into the story. Carruthers did not interrupt him. He sat looking into the fire, or else out towards the pale sunset. Between drags at his pipe he swallowed tea, but it was plain from his fixed expression that he was taking in every detail.

'And that's it,' Garth said finally, relaxing. 'I've got a few lines I'm following — orthodox work. But the really baffling parts I'm having to hand over to you.'

'Naturally,' Carruthers conceded. 'I assume you have reached a stage of mental development where you are capable of forming an opinion for yourself. Whom do you suspect in all this tangle?'

'I'm not sure . . . It's a toss-up between Sidney Laycock, Robert Alroyd and Leslie Gantry — with Victor de Maine-Kestrel hovering in the background.'

'Mmmm.' Carruthers chewed the end of his pipe-stem, his blue eyes hard in concentration. 'I don't see where Laycock fits in. Frankly, he doesn't fit at all. He's a chemist, a man of the world, and a nasty piece, of work to look at and talk to, according to you. Those sort are rarely criminals, but other people make use of their sub-human characteristics to make them *appear* so. Besides, he's right, you know.'

'In what way?' Garth asked, with a kind of formidable patience.

'In saying he wouldn't be such an idiot as to leave the clothes of his victim lying around for everybody to see. Of course he wouldn't! He'd chuck them in the acid bath with the body. And your own point is a reasonably good one — that the girl would not leave her fingerprints on the edge of the bath. No,' Carruthers concluded refreshingly, 'that whole set-up stinks. We can switch suspicion to Alroyd, Leslie Gantry, Kestrel, or Vera.'

'Or Vera?' Garth repeated. 'In what way?'

'I dunno, but something rings a bell somewhere.' Carruthers gave his impudent grin. 'Anyway, that's *your* part of the problem. You want me to look into the cage and the cause of Crafto's death, don't you?'

'That's it.' Garth assented, in some relief. 'Here's all I have concerning Crafto, and I can't help but think it means something.'

He brought forth stick-pin with its broken pearl and handed it over. Carruthers looked at it absently. Then:

'Crafto was lying face up, fully dressed, you said?'

'That's right. I don't believe he caught the pearl as he tried to drag his collar open, because had he done so the stock

154

tie would have dropped off. It was one of those clipped things.'

'I see. And there was an odd smell in the room where he'd died?'

'There was — a sort of stuffy smell. Suffocating, like gas of some sort.'

'And yet no traces of gas in the victim?'

'As to that, our surgeon is of the opinion there wasn't enough gas to leave a detectable trace.'

'That's possible, of course,' Carruthers admitted. 'All right, I'll take charge of this stick-pin and see what I can make of it. Now let's have a look at that specification of the cage which the engineer sent you.'

Garth handed it over, and with pipe crackling noisily the little scientist pored over the details. After perhaps five minutes of silent communion with himself he asked a question.

'I suppose the idea of a kind of spring blind never dawned on your addled pate?'

Whittaker and Garth glanced at each other.

'Why should it?' Garth demanded. 'What's a spring blind got to do with it?'

'Specifically, nothing, but this fifth bar

is modeled entirely on that principle, even to the nipples top and bottom. On to those nipples there could be placed something with slotted ends on the spring blind principle. Don't ask me what, because I haven't the least idea at this point — but it's a start. And of course you needn't waste time wondering how Vera got out of a cage like this. The thing's perfectly simple.'

'Glad to hear it,' Garth observed sourly. 'How did she get out, then?'

'She didn't. She was never *in*! Use your common-sense, man!'

Whittaker flashed a vaguely triumphant glance at this confirmation of his own assertion some time back.

'By no possible feat of contortion or phony magic could a living being get in or out of a cage like this,' Carruthers declared flatly, nearly stabbing through the sketch with the stem of his pipe. 'Dammit, the thing's solid all through. That is, if the real thing is identical with this plan.'

'It is identical, yes,' Garth confirmed. 'But if she was never in it why did everybody *see* her in it?'

'The eye,' Carruthers answered ambiguously, 'is a most fickle organ. It can't even show that train lines do not *really* meet, it just looks that way.'

'If it's all the same to you,' Garth said irritably, 'I'd rather we stuck to the point and not get involved with railway lines.'

Carruthers did not seem to be listening. He was still studying the sketch.

'These two holes in the base are interesting. Hardly be for ventilation,' he added, looking up and grinning.

'Hardly,' Garth conceded bitterly. 'As a matter of fact I have the feeling they may mean something definite, but I haven't the wit to imagine what.'

'Since they are not for ventilation,' Carruthers mused, 'and because a manufacturer of magical apparatus does not make mistakes, they must be for liquid of some kind. Did you move the cage around enough to discover if there was liquid in the base?'

'Good heavens, no! It never occurred to me.'

'Then it should have done! It is on these little points that never occur to you where you slip up so badly, otherwise you'd probably be a genius like me.'

Garth sighed, lighted a cheroot, and sat back in his chair.

'And the limelights were hot?' Carruthers murmured, his eyes narrow in thought.

'Extremely so,' Whittaker confirmed, as Garth seemed to have relapsed into injured silence.

'Hot limelights, possible liquid, holes for fluid to go into — mmm, all very interesting. I think when I see that cage that I shall have a definite line of approach.'

'Then I can leave that part of it to you?' Garth asked, breaking his silence.

'You can, yes. And I'll also examine this stick-pin and see if it tells anything. Your toxicologist may not have been dead right when he said there were no poison traces in the victim. I'm not finding fault with him, mind: I'm just pointing out that he can't possibly be as accurate as I am.'

Garth said nothing and Whittaker grinned privately to himself. Then Carruthers uncoiled himself from the chair and glanced at the clock.

'Since it's barely eight o'clock yet there's no reason why we shouldn't go and have a look at that cage now. I don't agree with delaying things like you fellows. Got your squad car with you?'

'We came by train,' Garth said.

'Then we'll have to go in mine. I'll just get my hat and coat.'

This did not take the little scientist above a few moments, then he led the way out to the garage, and his powerful racing car. Neither Garth nor Whittaker were particularly enthralled with the idea of being whirled back to London at a casual ninety miles an hour — which seemed to be Carruthers' concept of a cruising speed — but nevertheless it had to be done.

'Get in,' he ordered, when the car had been backed out of the garage, and stood waiting, a weird figure in his enormous overcoat and black homburg pushed to the back of his white-maned head.

Like schoolchildren before the head-master Garth and Whittaker obeyed, and then metaphorically held onto their breath as the whirlwind drive began. As usual Carruthers did not conform to street signs or traffic lights. With the law beside him in the car he simply tore up rules and regulations by the roots. And in consequence he screeched to a stop outside the immense Kestrel residence no more than thirty minutes later.

'This way,' Garth growled, his dyspepsia violently aggravated by fright.

In a few more minutes they were on the stage, the only other person present being the constable who had newly arrived on night duty. Carruthers glanced at him, then to Garth.

'What's the idea of him?' he questioned. 'Nothing else for the force to do?'

'Purely routine,' Garth replied. 'No knowing what may happen and I don't want this cage interfered with by outsiders.'

'Well, you can get rid of this blighter from here on. I'll be responsible for the cage.'

Garth gave a nod to the constable. 'Okay, you can report back to head-quarters.'

'Right, sir.'

Carruthers tugged off his hat, threw down his coat, and then glanced about him.

'Dark as hell on this stage. Get some lights on. Limelights as well. The whole issue.'

Whittaker moved to the switchboard and within seconds the stage and cage were brightly illuminated. Garth lighted a fresh cheroot, massaged his chest, and stood watching as Carruthers peered at the cage earnestly. After a moment he swung it back and forth and listened.

'Nothing liquid there,' Garth said, with a vague air of triumph.

'Not at the moment, I admit. Leave the limelights on and there may be.'

Whittaker raised an eyebrow at his superior, but neither of them passed any comment. Meanwhile Carruthers fiddled about with the mystery bar, watching the side open and shut at the touch of a finger.

'For your information,' he said after a moment, 'the inside of this bar is dewed over. Take a look.'

Garth and Whittaker did so, even though it did not explain anything to them.

'Condensation from the heat of these limelights?' Whittaker suggested.

'I hardly think so. The heat of the lamps is more likely acting upon the residue of a substance that has been in here. However, more of this later. We'll take a look at the limelights themselves.'

To climb up to them was a trifle to a man of Carruthers' agility but he swore volubly when the heat of the lamphouse stung his finger-ends.

'This is crazy!' he declared flatly. 'These lamps — since I suppose the twin is just as bad — should never be *this* hot. It's enough to burn 'em out.'

'Shall I switch 'em off?' Whittaker asked.

'You'd better. I didn't come up here to fry eggs!'

Whittaker departed and after a moment or two the limelights expired.

162

Carruthers fumed with impatience whilst he waited for the one beside him to cool down, then when it had done so he opened it up, studying it in the light of the battens.

'Lamp's all right, but far too high a rating for a limelight,' he announced. 'With these modern spots you can get all the brilliance of the old time carbon-arc from quite a low lamp rating — As for the excessive heat, the explanation's obvious. The heat filter has been taken out and the fan, usually in the top of the lamphouse, has been removed. See here . . . '

He indicated three bolts where some kind of fixture had been, and which neither Garth nor Whittaker had noticed on the previous occasion; then he pointed to the slots in the side of the lamphouse.

'I thought,' Garth said, glancing at Whittaker, 'that you said those slots were intended for gelatine color filters.'

'They're for both,' Carruthers explained. 'A heat filter is fixed in permanently, or should be, and there is still room to slide the gelatine color filters over the top of them.'

'Which indicates,' Garth said slowly, 'that somebody deliberately removed all means of cooling the beam from these two spots?'

'Precisely. And the reason? To give enough heat onto that cage to cause something to melt . . . That reminds me, put those limes on again, Whittaker. I want to see what reaction we get from that bar.'

Whittaker complied, and presently Garth and Carruthers joined him on the stage again. Immediately the little scientist went over to the cage and inspected the still open trap-tube.

'The temporary shutting off of the limelights doesn't seem to have slowed things up too much,' he commented. 'See what you think of it now.'

Dutifully, Whittaker and Garth looked, puzzled by the brightly reflective 'sweat' which was visible from nipple to nipple inside the tube.

'What *is* it?' Garth demanded. 'Grease, or wet, or what?'

'No idea yet, but it's something highly reflective which has a very low melting point. Maybe something with a mercury base . . . ' He seized the cage and swung it back and forth. This time, much to the surprise of the two Yard men, there was a distinct plopping, lobbing sound, like the smack of water under a pier. Since there would be no *depth* of liquid in the base of the cage, the only other solution was *heaviness*.

'Lovely!' Carruthers beamed. 'Things are working out just as I anticipated. How rare it is for my genius to be incorrect.'

From his jacket pocket he took a bulky affair of leather rather like a cigar case and extracted a small, spoon-like instrument.

'Get this cage tilted until liquid comes out of those holes,' he instructed, and this was a job for Whittaker. The only way he could do it was by using a spare rope from the flies, fastening it to the cage at the side opposite the holes, then returning to the flies and hauling on the rope until the cage was nearly up-ended. Only then did a brightly glittering liquid, with all the heaviness of mercury but with a much more glassy content, begin to pour

forth like thick cream. Carruthers col-
lected a 'spoonful' and then set it aside to
solidify.

'Right, off with the lights!' he ordered.
'And drop the cage back into position.'

This was duly done and Garth raised
an enquiring eyebrow.

'What happens now, Doc?'

'Nothing. I'll check that stuff in my
laboratory. When I know what it is we'll
have taken a giant stride towards the
solution of Vera Kestrel's disappearance
— And that reminds me! Where is the
cover which was put over this cage?'

'Here,' Whittaker said, bringing it in
from the wings and dumping it down.

Carruthers began to examine it, a task
that did not take him above a few
moments. He was grinning rather sardonically as he straightened up again.

'Fireproof,' he announced. 'Not exactly
asbestos because that would be too stiff,
but something very much like it. And the
reason? To block the heat of the spotlights
whilst jiggery-pokery went on.'

'So far,' Garth said, belching thunder-
ously and forgetting to excuse himself,

'you're doing fine. But what about the voice? My suspicion is one of those pocketsized loud-speakers.'

'A suspicion quite justified. What more do you want?'

'To give the impression of the voice coming from the cage the voice would obviously have to come from that quarter of the stage, via a loudspeaker. My idea is that the loudspeaker was suspended from the flies and then pulled upwards and away quickly after the trick was performed. I've good reason for thinking so: there's a broken ventilator grating which looks as though something has been pulled through it in a hurry. The broken pieces of lattice point upwards.'

'We'll look,' Carruthers decided, and for the second time made the ascent, this time into the false roof. He studied each point as Garth gave it and at length nodded.

'No reason why your idea shouldn't be right,' he assented. 'But to where was the loudspeaker *connected?* That's a vital point. There must have been a microphone through which Vera presumably spoke. I'm only on the edge of things as yet: there is a whole lot more I want.'

'You're welcome to it,' Garth grinned. 'What do you propose?'

'Having sandwiches and tea sent in and spend the rest of tonight prowling and thinking — alone. I can do wonders when there are no untrained minds present to keep interrupting me with useless babblings.'

'All right, if that's how you want it,' Garth said huffily. 'The untrained minds will take themselves off and leave you to it. You'll let me know when anything develops?'

'Naturally — and I shall expect you to do the same for me.'

Garth jerked his head and with Whittaker beside him left the residence.

'Damned upstart,' he muttered, as Whittaker led the way to the nearest 'bus stop. 'Thinks he knows everything!'

'He pretty well does, sir, which is why he can afford to be so cocky . . . Anyway, what is our next move? It's half-past nine,' Whittaker added hopefully.

'I know it, and I can't think of anything

which won't keep until tomorrow morning. We can part here, Whitty, and rejoin forces after a sleep. Perhaps by that time the great ex-backroom boy will have discovered something . . . '

★　★　★

There was, however, no report waiting for Garth at his office the following morning — not from Hiram Carruthers anyway; but on the other hand the handwriting and fingerprint experts had evidently been busy and had sent in detailed statements in full. His digestion fighting with bacon and egg, Garth picked up the fingerprint report and scowled through it. It stated briefly that the fingerprints on the hairbrush supplied tallied in every particular with those on the murder weapons, and acid bath sides. They were Vera Main-Kestrel's.

'That doesn't make me any more sure that she's dead,' Garth grunted, glancing at Whittaker. 'You've seen these?'

'I have, sir, yes. The report on the informer's note is particularly interesting.'

Garth sat down and read it, lighting a cheroot meanwhile.

Department of Calligraphy Report

In our opinion the note submitted and signed by 'Informer' has been executed in logwood ink. This dries purplish black, changing to pure black. It has been written recently and, we submit, not by a person so uneducated as it is intended to convey. The word 'laboratory', by no means an easy word to spell for an uneducated person, is given correctly each time. On the other hand words like 'burglar' and 'pestered' are misspelled — one feels with deliberation. The paper upon which the note has been written is quite good quality stuff, and a fountain pen with a very smooth nib was used for the writing, none of which conforms with a down-and-out type of cat burglar of little education.

The backwardly-slanted characters are often used by the inexperienced to disguise their natural handwriting, and the same mistake is obvious here. The general smallness of the writing is rarely found executed by a man, so our theoretical conclusions are that the note has been written by a woman, or else a man with an exceptionally effeminate streak.

'As you say,' Garth commented, 'very interesting. And not altogether unexpected so far as I'm concerned.'

'You have a theory then, sir?'

'Of course I have! You don't think I haven't given this business a good deal of meditation, do you? Here's my view — that since she was never in the cage, Vera escaped somehow after conveying the impression that she *was* in the cage. She made a complete get-away by a means we haven't yet discovered. She then went to Sidney Laycock's laboratory — and without his knowledge, I imagine, since he'd hardly be a party to something that might lead to his conviction for murder. After she got there she left all her clothes and arranged a set-up which looked as though she'd been done away with in acid, and faked a note which was sent to me by being put in the letter-box — the Yard letter-box, I mean — either by her or somebody she paid to do it.'

'In other words a deliberate deflection of guilt onto Sidney Laycock?'

'Why not? She and Laycock hardly adored each other in spite of their intention to marry, and she was in love with Robert Alroyd. She may have had some very cogent reason for wishing Laycock to get it in the neck.'

'Uh-huh, it hangs together,' Whittaker admitted. 'She'd also have the chance to get an impression of the laboratory key from Laycock. As his fiancée she was with him a good deal. She could have chosen an ideal moment to quickly get the key impression she wanted, even under some pretext of a job to be done wherein Laycock had to remove his jacket. That wouldn't baffle a woman of her resource.'

'Also,' Garth mused, 'it makes sense of her call here to ask for police protection. Knowing what she was going to do — if we assume my theory to be right — she knew the police would investigate. After allowing a respectable amount of time to elapse she performed the 'Informer' gag. She'd know we'd have to follow it up, even if we didn't believe it. Her amateur touch is revealed by her not making sure first that the laboratory was a spot through which a burglar would have to pass to reach either of the adjoining houses. The note was addressed to me, even though she hadn't met me, but from the papers she'd know I was in charge of the case.'

'She also knew you are the boss here because she asked for you when she first arrived.'

'And where is she now and how did she do it?' Garth mused, one eye shut against cheroot smoke. 'Who is Leslie Gantry to whom she paid two hundred and fifty thousand pounds so easily? These damned banks! If only they'd give us a tumble . . . '

'Leslie Gantry apart, sir, we'd probably get on a lot better if we could locate Robert Alroyd. Since he's her true lover, and gone abroad, I'd be willing to stake even money that she's with him.'

Garth reflected for a moment, then made up his mind and snapped on the intercom.

'I've an idea,' he said, as Whittaker gave his enquiring glance. 'I'm going to have Vera's picture carried a whole lot further than just to our own airports and railway stations. I'm going to have the French Sureté and other European police get on the job of trying to find her. And Canada and the United States, too!'

Whittaker nodded and waited whilst Garth gave his orders over the intercom, then he picked up the telephone as it jangled noisily.

'Chief-Inspector Garth's office.'

'Put him on,' ordered the irate voice of Hiram Carruthers.

Whittaker grinned and handed the 'phone across, murmuring 'Beethoven' as he did so.

'Hello there, Doc,' Garth exclaimed, feeling momentarily genial as his dyspepsia faded. 'How's things going?'

'Perfectly, of course. What else did you expect? You'll have to come over to my place and see a demonstration. And don't keep me waiting. When do I expect you?'

Garth glanced at his watch. 'I could manage it by the next train, but I must be back in London this afternoon to attend the Crafto inquest.'

'Very well. This morning.' The line became dead, and Garth put the 'phone down.

'Do I come with you, sir?' Whittaker asked.

'Yes, you might as well. Sometimes I don't have the vaguest idea what our backroom genius is talking about whereas you do. When's the next train to Halingford?'

Whittaker looked it up. 'Ten-twenty-eight, sir. We can just about make it.'

Garth got to his feet, considered, and then nodded to himself.

'Hop over to the pathology department, will you, and pick up that knife and hacksaw from them? I'm not casting aspersions on their conclusions but Carruthers may be able to find something more than they did with the instruments he's got.'

Whittaker nodded and departed, joining Garth as he was about to leave the building. They caught the 10-28 in ample time and arrived in Carruthers' atrociously untidy den towards 11-30. From the domestic regions of the great Georgian house there wafted the tingling odor of frying onions.

'Any tea?' Carruthers asked, a big mug of it in front of him as he sat at his paper-littered desk.

'No thanks,' Garth responded hurriedly. 'Just how far have you got, Doc? I don't want to rush you but — '

'You're not *going* to rush me; I'll see to that. If I once begin to gulp my tea I'll start suffering from your complaint. Sit down, both of you. You shouldn't be tired, though, seeing as you've probably slept like logs all night. I haven't. I only got back from the Kestrel place at eight this morning, and since then I've had a lot to do.'

'You actually mean there was enough to keep you going all night?' Garth asked in amazement.

'There was — and for once in my life

I'm indebted to you for throwing in my lap the most amazing set-up ever. It amounts to near-genius. In fact it must do otherwise I wouldn't have had such difficulty solving it.'

'Then you know where Vera is?' Whittaker asked eagerly.

'Why should I?'

'But I thought you said — '

'Concentrate on what I *did* say, boy. I never mentioned her. I know how her vanishing act was performed, and I know how Crafto died. Those were my two assignments in this problem, and I've finished them . . .'

Carruthers put down his empty tea-mug, blew out his cheeks, then got to his feet. 'Come with me, you two . . .'

He shuffled out of his study and led the way below into his laboratory, every detail of it brilliantly lighted by shadowless floods.

'Firstly, to the matter of Crafto,' he said, lighting his briar. 'I want you to witness a small demonstration. I have here a dummy man, adorned in a stock-tie, with a complete pearl-headed stick-pin. Observe.'

He pulled aside a dustsheet from a dummy and Whittaker and Garth stood looking at it.

'For the purposes of our experiment, that is Crafto,' he explained. 'Just as he must have looked in his room before being murdered. Now, watch carefully . . . '

The Yard men did not need telling twice. Anything which Caruthers performed in the way of experiments always fascinated them, and this was no exception. He crossed to the furthest point of the laboratory and tinkered about for a few moments with an apparatus rather like a small portable radio, except that it was a good deal more complicated. Finally he switched it on and from it there came a faint buzzing note.

'Now,' the little scientist instructed, 'keep your eyes on the stick-pin pearl.'

Garth and Whittaker did so, and to their surprise they saw the pearl abruptly smash to pieces as Carruthers turned a potentiometer on the apparatus. Grinning, he switched off again and sucked pensively at his briar.

7

'The expression on your faces is well worth recording,' he commented, after a moment. 'I'm sorry I haven't a camera all set up.'

'What sort of a gag did you pull just then?' Garth demanded. 'Vibration?'

'In a sense. Ultrasonic waves to be exact, of a pitch too low to affect human physical structure, but none the less sharp enough to cause a brittle object like an imitation pearl to shatter. If necessary the ultrasonic waves could be generated over a distance of several miles. I'll let you in on a secret. There's a device at the War Office very similar to this, patented of course, and being held in readiness for that Third War when it comes.'

'Patented?' Garth interrupted. 'Wait a minute! I do believe I've got an idea — '

'Namely that Robert Alroyd was a Patentees' Agent and could have seen the plan of a device like this and copied it? Yes, I thought of that too, and that's probably what he did do. Why not? Since he didn't market the thing in the ordinary way he didn't infringe the patent as such. He turned it to a diabolical use of his own. For the moment, though, that is beside the point. The smashing of the pearl in the stick-pin is only half the story. Note the position of the stick-pin — directly under the nostrils of the wearer, and the wearer was Crafto . . . '

Carruthers strolled forward and from the desk picked up the original broken stick-pin which Garth had given him. Then he continued:

'I analysed this thing with the electron microscope, and the spectrograph. From the latter I received enough color reaction to discover traces of phosgene gas, sometimes known as chlorocarbonic acid gas, or oxychloride of carbon. It is colorless and deadly poisonous. The smallest cubic quantity of it if directly inhaled can bring about almost instant suffocation. It leaves behind a heavy, graveyard smell — which was undoubtedly the odor you noticed in Crafto's room.'

'Then it means,' Garth said grimly, 'that somebody filled the pearl on the stickpin with phosgene gas and then, at their pleasure, smashed the pearl with ultrasonic waves? Crafto got a good inhalation of it being directly under his nose and died as a result. That it?'

'That's it. Somebody kept watch for him going to his room, I suppose. They could even have been on the other side of the street. They switched on the ultrasonic apparatus — which would not need to be big and could be battery-operated if it was only to operate over a short distance — and the outflowing vibration did the rest. It passed through the walls of the apartment house and shattered the brittle pearl at Crafto's throat. Any other brittle object would have smashed too, only there didn't happen to be any in the room.'

'Which meant nobody needed to enter the room at all except Crafto himself?' Whittaker gave a half admiring smile.

'That's turning science to murderous account with a vengeance.'

'Most expert criminals do so these days,' Carruthers said.

'There's a point here though that needs clearing up,' Garth mused. 'When would anybody get the chance to fill Crafto's pearl pin with gas?'

'I've thought that one out,' Carruthers said, an insolent droop on his eyelids. 'Apparently — from your report, Whittaker — Crafto rid himself of his suit and stocktie to perform the vanishing trick. He was dressed as a wizard, or something. In that time his stock tie must have been in the dressing-room. It was only of the conventional clip-on type and therefore could be easily duplicated. I suggest that the murderer had seen him on the halls and knew that in parts of his act he rid himself of his immaculate suit and stock-tie, and that that would be the moment to act. Crafto did not perform his vanishing trick on the halls, I gather, since the Kestrel demonstration was the first one. However, he had evidently given the clue that he did at some point rid himself of his stock-tie. Very well — all the killer had to do was prepare a duplicate pin with gas in the faked pearly head and stick it in a duplicate stock-tie. The switch was done whilst the magician was in his wizard's outfit.'

'Then the killer must have performed the switch at the Kestrel's whilst people were in the wings?' Garth demanded.

'There were only two in the wings — the two chorus girls, and they have admitted they were watching the *act*. It is a logical assumption that they were so much absorbed by the illusion they never even glimpsed the unknown who flitted in and out to Crafto's dressing-room. We must admit that the killer took a long chance on not being seen, but evidently he timed it beautifully and got away with it. Crafto put on the fatal stock-tie unaware that thereafter he must have been shadowed constantly . . . And I think we may take it for granted that Robert Alroyd is the one we're seeking because he had access to the plans of countless inventions. He may even have had this murder scheme in mind for months and made a copy of all inventions likely to help him in his master-scheme when he launched it.'

'It's cunning,' Garth muttered. 'Damn me if it isn't!'

'Which, I fancy, disposes of him,' Carruthers commented.

'There's an inquest this afternoon.' Garth said. 'Maybe I should submit this evidence then?'

'Why rush in? Better to astound the lot of 'em with the *full* story — and I haven't nearly finished yet. Look, I want you to come over to the Kestrel place and see the reenactment of the vanishing act. You're not *compelled* to be at the inquest: it will be adjourned anyway pending further enquiry. Wouldn't you rather see how the rest of the problem works out?'

Garth nodded. 'Okay then. They have my report that can be read at the inquest. I've sufficient justification for being absent if I'm collecting important evidence. Oh, before we go. I've got a knife and hacksaw here that have been examined by forensic, and they claim the presence of human tissue. I'm not doubting it, but I'd like a double check.'

Whittaker handed over the knife and hacksaw, and Carruthers looked at them thoughtfully.

'From the Laycock laboratory, I suppose?'

'Correct,' Garth assented. 'If that tissue *is* human I'm led to the uncomfortable possibility that we may be up the wrong alley after all. The tissue could belong to Vera, yet without a specimen tissue or blood drop from her herself we can't fix anything definite, only work on assumption.'

'Assumption has no place in an investigator's *modus operandi*,' Carruthers said. 'We work only on facts. Tell me something: how big is the acid bath in the Laycock lab?'

'About ten feet long by three across.'

'Then in that case I don't think it signifies very much *what* we find in the way of tissue or bloodstains. It is a glaring case of gilding the lily. Clinging to your original assumption that Vera Kestrel may have engineered all this to plant guilt on Laycock, we see signs of her having overdone it. First we have the fingerprints on the edge of the acid bath, and now we have tissue and bloodstains to point to possible dismemberment. But I ask you, why dismember a body when you've got a bath ten feet long? There arises no necessity to indulge in butchery.'

'That's certainly something I hadn't thought of,' Garth admitted.

'I'll have a look anyhow,' Carruthers decided, and immediately went to work with the electron microscope. Evidently not entirely satisfied with what he beheld here he extended his analysis to chemical reactions and finally considered a test-tube filled with a muddy white substance.

'Forensic are entirely correct,' he confirmed. 'Blood Group O and traces of human tissue on knife and hacksaw teeth. Very unconvincing. An expert chemist who has just done a dismemberment would make a better job of cleaning his tools than *that*!'

'True, but — ' Garth looked puzzled. 'Where do you suppose the human tissues came from?'

'Vera of course — providing we still

assume she engineered this job. She wouldn't be above damaging herself to provide the evidence. A chunk from her arm or leg, where it doesn't show, would be sufficient. By a 'chunk,' I mean, of course, a deliberate hacking of the flesh to produce the desired effect. What a pity it's so overdone because without contrary proof this could be built up as circumstantial evidence to hang Laycock. It is the over-elaboration which makes one look further.'

'I have to admit you're an invaluable help, Doc,' Garth sighed, as Whittaker put the knife and hacksaw back in the envelope.

'About time you realized it.' Carruthers grinned sardonically and glanced at his watch. 'Well, gentlemen, I think we'd better hop into London in my car, by which time we'll be ready for lunch. Then we'll carry on to the Kestrel place, and I'll see if I can astound you further. Agreed?'

'Definitely,' Garth assented.

'Right. I've one or two things to collect material to my demonstration, then we'll be on our way . . . '

It was two o'clock when the three arrived at the Kestrel home, Garth having obtained the sanction of the A.C. over the 'phone to skip the inquest since he was following an important line of evidence. The theatre-ballroom was entirely deserted and had a peculiarly forlorn look in the cloudy afternoon sunlight. Nothing had apparently been disturbed. The cage was still hanging where it had been left, but of course the guardian constable was no longer present. Carruthers, carrying with him a long cylindrical object wrapped in oilproof paper, led the way to the stage and mounted to it, then he whipped off his overcoat and threw his homburg after it.

'Lights, but not limes,' he instructed briefly, and Whittaker went to the switchboard to comply. Carruthers nodded and then gave his slow, mysterious smile.

'You are about to witness the supreme peak of my genius,' he explained solemnly. 'Commencing with this . . .'

From the oilproof paper he produced an object like a rolled-up blind, having a socket at each end. Quite deliberately he fixed this to the nipples within Bar five, one end of the 'blind' being on an in-sunken spring which allowed for it to spring back tightly into place.

'Clear so far?' he questioned, and Garth nodded as he drew hard on his cheroot. Whittaker watched from nearby, completely absorbed.

'This bar — the part that is slotted and now fitted with this spring roller device — is five feet ten inches long,' Carruthers continued. 'In other words, amply high enough to accommodate the height of Vera Kestrel, who was. I gather, around five feet four inches tall?'

'Around that,' Whittaker confirmed, wondering vaguely what was coming next.

'Now — observe something,' Carruthers continued, and with a practiced flip of his fingers he caused the spring-blind affair to suddenly open — so suddenly indeed that both Garth and Whittaker stared back. They had never for a moment expected what they now beheld — the entire back of the cage's interior covered with a slightly curving screen as reflective as glass.

'So far, so good,' Carruthers said, enjoying himself immensely. 'Now, gentlemen, go into the main hall there and watch what happens next. You, Whittaker, will know if it resembles the disappearance of Vera Kestrel. The only thing different will be that I shan't use the heat-proof cloth as cover.'

Garth and Whittaker departed hurriedly, and by the time they looked around again Carruthers had disappeared. Then the two spotlights came into being, throwing the cage into immense brilliance — but this was not all. Carruthers himself was in the cage, bowing cynically, and waving a hand.

'You observe me?' he asked. 'Apparently well and securely trapped?'

'Yes, the illusion's perfect,' Garth cried. 'Even your voice is coming from the right place!'

'So it should. I wired everything up in the night, including the spotlights, so I can operate them from a distance. Now watch what happens to me in the cage. It may take a few moments . . . '

There was a tense interval, then Carruthers began to fade mysteriously in the cage, until at length there was a dispersing mist, vapor of some kind, and he was no longer there.

'That's it!' Whittaker exclaimed. 'That's exactly what happened to Vera!'

Immediately he began hurrying towards the stage, Garth beside him, and after a while Carruthers rejoined them, coming from the wings and grinning mysteriously. The spotlights were now out.

'Satisfactory?' he asked.

'Terrific!' Garth exclaimed, staring at the cage. 'And I'll be damned if there's a single clue.'

'There would be if you swung the cage. You'd hear the liquefied mirror sloshing around in the cage base. Naturally, not knowing what to look for, nobody touched the cage — and in five minutes, with the spotlights off, the stuff will have solidified.'

'What stuff?' Garth asked, baffled. 'What's this about a liquefied mirror?'

'I'm coming to it. Give me time, man, can't you? The spring screen that you saw was, I believe, an exact duplicate of the type of spring screen used by Crafto. It is made on the same principle as a roller blind and is the basis of many magical illusions. Its edges are actually straight, of exceedingly strong tension, which causes them to flatten out rigidly when contrary pressure is released. Rather like those steel things women used to wear in corsets.'

'Uh-huh,' Garth acknowledged. 'My own missus still uses 'em in hers. But go on — '

'The spring-screen was imprisoned within the hollow bar and released by a catch. When this happened the two side pieces, made of spring, stretched forth a fine network of bendable rollable material called gustin. If you've never heard of that read up on the science of rubber extraction and you'll find it is a product little used commercially because of its very low melting point. In basis it *is* rubber, but at a temperature of one hundred Fahrenheit degrees or over it deliquesces. You're still following me?'

'Right on the beam,' Garth agreed, smoking fiercely.

'Very well. On this bendable sheet of basic rubber, its edges made taut by the thin springs, we find a covering of mercuroid. Mercuroid in its pure state is basically mercury, which again has a low melting point and an extremely high reflective power. Mercuroid is used in the mirrors of the world's most important telescopes, and in its what I will call inferior state, can be used like a paint and sprayed. That is what happened here. Low melting point, high reflective value. The result of spraying the poor grade mercuroid onto the gustin sheet produced a very passable mirror — but with the one fault, from a normal point of view that is, that it would melt in a temperature above one hundred degrees. It did — the mercuroid and gustin together, the liquid flowing into the two holes in the cage base and there solidifying when the spotlights were turned off. I deduced the

193

gustin and mercuroid from analysis of the slight deposits left behind in this hollow bar, and of course from the material in the base of the cage. Crafto, no doubt, was well rehearsed in the art of being able to touch the master bar with his wand at exactly the right spot. I had to use my hands, but with practice I could produce as good an illusion as he must have done.'

'Fair enough so far,' Garth acknowledged. 'But what about the side-springs? They wouldn't melt, would they? When the gustin and mercuroid flowed off, what happened to the side springs which had been supporting the material?'

'As far as I can tell, once the supporting material *had* melted away the side springs were left unsupported and dropped as straight, wafer-thin slats to the base of the cage. Crafto, amidst the vapors produced by the dissolution of the mercuroid, could easily move those and put them in his wizard's gown out of sight. You see, the only thing holding the springs apart and tightly onto the nipples — when the mirror screen was rolled up I mean — was the screen itself. When it melted the side pieces naturally had nothing to hold them and must have dropped. As expert an illusionist as Crafto would very easily find a convenient moment to whip away two nearly two-dimensional slats of about four feet length before anybody noticed it. Particularly as nobody was looking for it.'

Garth dropped his cheroot and screwed his heel on it. 'But that's only half the story, surely? Where *was* Vera when this happened?'

'There . . . ' Carruthers nodded towards the right-hand pillar at the side of the stage, that bulging creation of imitation granite. Garth looked at it and frowned.

'How the devil could she be? She'd be seen.'

'Not the way that pillar's devised. Notice its position? From the audience it is not visible because the curtains, even when drawn fully back, cover it completely. It can only be seen fully from this stage. The same applies to the pillar on the other side, but that doesn't signify since it is harmless.'

'And this one isn't?' Whittaker questioned.

Carruthers lighted his pipe before replying. 'These pillars, in case you don't know it, are movable. They work on chains from the false roof. I imagine they're movable so that, if need be, they can be shifted to stage center to stand as colonnades for some classic play or other.'

'We found that out,' Garth said. 'Only we monkeyed around with that *other* pillar — not this one.'

'That's a pity, otherwise you'd have tumbled to a quite clever trick.' Carruthers grinned and then asked:

'Ever hear of the old 'Pass, pass, bottle and glass' trick in which a cover is put over a bottle, it disappears, and a wineglass or something else turns up in its place?'

'Old as the hills,' Whittaker said in contempt.

'Old it may be, son, but this particular pillar utilizes the same principle! Stay here and watch something.'

He wandered across the stage and then mounted the ladder that led to the false roof. Presently he disappeared and there came the faint, hardly distinguishable whine of an electric motor.

'For the love of Mike, look!' Whittaker gasped, pointing.

Garth *was* looking, more surprised than he had ever been in his investigative career. For a thin line was running swiftly and soundlessly up the guilty pillar — horizontally across it — and within a matter of seconds it became obvious how this queer, swift effect was produced. A shell was rising swiftly from the pillar proper, and when this shell was three-quarters to the pillar's summit it stopped, revealing in the genuine pillar, which was hollow, an opening six feet high by three broad and edged around with light bulbs which were gleaming brightly.

Into this brightly lighted 'pocket' Carruthers presently ascended, evidently by way of a ladder from below, pushing up a trapdoor in the floor of the 'pocket' to do so.

'Happy?' he enquired cynically, as Whittaker and Garth stared up at his brilliantly lighted figure.

'Hysterical,' Garth responded. 'A shell pillar, I take it?'

'That's right, and I'll show you the exact working afterward. For the moment, if your brains can stand it, I'd prefer you to concentrate on a matter of angles. You will please notice that this opening in the pillar is exactly diagonal to the stage center. Take 'X' as your mental plan and the center of the X represents the center of the stage. I am at the foot of the right-hand X-cross. You gather that?'

'Just about,' Garth muttered.

'Add to that bright lighting turned inwards which illuminates me but *not* the stage, and picture your mirror at the center of the stage inside the cage, and what do you get? You get a reflection of me from any point in the hall whereas I myself am invisible! When the mirror melts I vanish from sight naturally, and whilst the confusion and interest is at its height I touch a button in this little alcove here and down slides the outer shell-pillar, its line of movement masked from the audience by the curtains. Visible to Crafto, yes, but then he was in the know.

Invisible in the wings also . . . A matter of reflection from start to finish.'

'Damned cunning, these Chinese,' Whittaker commented.

'How does that pillar work?' Garth demanded. 'I can't understand how we missed it.'

'You missed it for two reasons: One, you weren't looking for any monkey business with a pillar, and second, by mischance, you happened to investigate the other pillar and assumed the other would be like it. That's where you went wrong. Come up and I'll show you.'

The Yard men wasted no time in complying. They joined Carruthers eventually in the false roof, though it was something of a puzzle to them how he got there. He appeared to follow them from below, and at the moment of his arrival they were gazing at the great pillar-shell drawn to its limit in the top of the false roof, suspended by a chain operated by an electric winch perched on a high and solid platform.

'Well, you should have looked further, eh?' Carruthers asked, batting the dust from himself. 'You investigated that other pillar over there, I take it?'

'And raised it a little by the hand winch,' Whittaker confirmed. 'We saw this pillar top, of course, like a turntable, with a ring in the center, and *also* chained to a hand-winch. We didn't see that other electric winch in the higher parts of the roof, which is now holding the shell up.'

'For the simple reason,' Carruthers said, 'that somebody must have been up here — an assistant to Vera, I imagine, and maybe Crafto too — who cleared away the evidences at lightning speed when the trick had been performed. The shell, when it had dropped down, was unhooked and the chain drawn up to the limit of the overhead winch. The normal hand-winch chain was put in its place and the unknown vacated through there . . . '

Carruthers nodded to a distant part of the vast false roof area where, it was noticeable, there were bricks which looked curiously out of pattern.

'That's a door, painted with imitation brick inside, and leading to a fire-escape outside,' Carruthers explained. 'It drops down to one of the main paths at the back of the house. You didn't investigate the outside of this place half enough, you know.'

'I hadn't time,' Garth growled. 'I sent one of my men and he couldn't find anything. Should have done it myself . . . But this pillar business — I see how the shell works, and I suppose it's operated from inside the 'pocket' by means of an electric switch?'

'Which moves the shell swiftly and soundlessly up or down, yes. The electric winch is controlled from the 'pocket', as you aptly call it. Entrance to the 'pocket' is made up a ladder inside the genuine pillar, which — although it is movable if need be — nonetheless fits over a deep well. That well leads to a short underground passage and finally ascends stone steps to a trap-door amidst the shrubbery edging the kitchen garden at the back of the house. On top of the trap is a cucumber frame, which exactly fits it. Possibly the head gardener knows all about it but is paid well enough to keep quiet — which again leads us to put complete suspicion on Vera Kestrel.'

'But,' Garth said hazily, 'we looked for a passageway trap and couldn't find one.'

'I assume you descended in the wings into the normal passage which goes beneath the stage? The passage I'm talking about goes the *opposite* way. The wall of the well is the wall of the normal passage, so obviously you didn't see anything. Imagine a letter 'L'. Now, the upright is the well below the pillar, and the right-hand horizontal base stroke is the passage leading out to the kitchen garden. The normal under-stage passage is on the left side of the 'L' upright and therefore seems complete in itself.'

Garth popped a magnesia tablet in his mouth and reflected, his eyes screwed up.

'One day I'll sit down and work all this out. I gather the drift, but it needs thinking about.'

'All my investigations need thinking about,' Carruthers grinned. 'But all this is true. What happened, I imagine, was that Vera — again assuming it was she — when she went off-stage before the trick actually slipped outside to the kitchen garden, went swiftly through the second passage, and emerged into her 'pocket' in the pillar. She pressed the switch which made the shell rise. Up in the false roof here her assistant was keeping watch to be sure everything worked without fail. Vera then put on the inwardly turned lights of the pocket, put a rope about herself to make it look as if she were bound, and just stood. Crafto did the rest with hot limelight and liquid glass and gustin. Above Vera, out of sight of her reflection, would be a mike, connected to the speaker in the flies. An amplifier must certainly have been used, and presumably the assistant took charge of that too. It would not have to be very big . . . So the stage was set and Vera did her act. The instant 'dissolution' had taken place she set the shell pillar dropping and raced back down the passage to the kitchen garden, and after that to wherever she *did* go. Her assistant up here did the rest. I fancy he had trouble getting the speaker away quickly and smashed the vent in doing it. But get away he *did*, leaving everything as planned — comparatively neat and tidy. After which he presumably joined Vera.'

'I suggest,' Whittaker put in, thinking hard, 'that he did not join her immediately but came back and seized his chance to switch Crafto's stock-tie. Meantime Vera possibly re-dressed herself somewhere — even in the summer-house in the grounds — and then went on to Laycock's laboratory and left her clothes in full sight on a peg. When the police didn't bite at that lead she sent a note to get things started.'

'And in the laboratory provided the fingerprints, tissue, bloodstains, and what-have-you,' Garth said slowly. 'Yes, that seems reasonable enough. And the assistant?'

Carruthers shrugged. 'That isn't my part of the job now I've solved the mechanics — but I'd suggest Robert Alroyd, Vera's genuine lover. Once again, he may have used the basis of an invention he'd seen to work out all this pillar business. It is perfectly clear now that this matter has been planned out over a long time and executed in comparative secrecy. I don't suppose there was much interruption either since Mr. Kestrel himself plainly considered Vera a spoiled child who must have a theatre-ballroom for her amusement. He probably didn't care *what* she did, which would make her whole plan easier.'

'I'll wager Alroyd thought out most of it,' Garth declared. 'I recall that in his letter to her he said something about her proposition not going nearly far enough — which was probably when she mentioned this plan for the first time. Yes, I'll gamble he was the master behind most of it.'

Garth thumped his chest violently, belched, and then lighted a fresh cheroot.

'Vast elaboration — to what end?' He gave the little scientist a dour look.

'That's plain enough, isn't it? To pin Sidney Laycock down as her murderer. She has some deep and bitter hatred against him, and I wouldn't mind gambling that it's connected with that Michael Ayrton case of long ago. This may not be a case of a woman scorned,

Garth, but it's something in the same category.'

'Would you consider that two hundred and fifty thousand pounds is a big sum to pay — say, Robert Alroyd, for fixing up all this stunt?'

'I'd say it was daylight robbery,' Carruthers replied blandly. 'I gather you're suggesting that Leslie Gantry may be Alroyd's assumed name as the recipient of a check?'

'Seems logical.'

'Surely — but try something else,' Carruthers grinned. 'If you had planned a perfect disappearance and did not intend to ever return you'd automatically cut yourself off from your bank account, wouldn't you? Well, Vera's done the same thing — but being a wealthy woman she can throw two hundred and fifty thousand around like confetti — so what does she do? I suggest she pays the money to *herself* somewhere, using the name of Leslie Gantry. She won't need to turn up as a man to collect on her deposit, remember. There are a lot of *girls* named Leslie.'

'I'll be thrice damned,' Garth swore. 'Why didn't I think of that?'

The physicist shrugged. 'You're Garth and I'm Carruthers, that's why.'

'And Crafto was evidently put out of the way in case he revealed too much?' Whittaker asked.

'As to that — ' Carruthers reflected for a moment. 'As to that, I've given a lot of thought to your statement that he seemed genuinely upset when Vera did not reappear. I believe he did not know she intended to genuinely vanish for good. I think he was engaged purely to perform his illusion, and no doubt he never performed it before on a stage because of the pillar problem. On the other hand. Alroyd may have worked out the whole cage business from inventions he had seen, and Crafto was employed to put the thing over because he had the stage technique and could put over other stunts as well. Now, assuming he knew the whole set-up of the trick, which indeed he must have done, and yet did *not* know that Vera intended to vanish for good, he must have been genuinely horrified when she failed to turn up. It also made him a dangerous witness because he knew all the answers. His stubborn refusal to divulge the trick may have been because he wanted to contact Vera, or Alroyd, first and find out what was going on. And because he knew too much he was eliminated. It's a guess, but I think it's correct — as my few guesses invariably are.'

'Yes,' Garth mused, 'I think you're on the beam there, but we can only be sure when we've contacted Vera herself, or else Alroyd. Somehow we've *got* to do so, otherwise the plot laid around Sidney Laycock will develop as Vera has designed, and he's liable to be convicted on the evidence provided — '

'I've been thinking, sir,' Whittaker put in, 'even that gold tooth-shell of Vera's was evidently coldly premeditated as a part of the plan. She knew most people would notice it — and she made a particular point of allowing it to show when she talked to me back at the Yard — so evidently the reason for that was to draw attention to it in the bottom of the acid bath.'

'All of which adds up to the fact that dear little Vera is quite an astute little girl,' Carruthers commented; then he glanced at his watch. 'Mmmm — time flies. I'm in need of my four o'clock cup of tea. Will you gentlemen join me at the nearest café?'

'Glad to,' Garth growled. 'I've got the devil's own gripe.'

They descended again to the stage, and Carruthers slipped into his overcoat and picked up his hat.

'I'm wondering,' Garth said, as they left the theatre-ballroom, 'do you think old man Kestrel has any stake in all this?'

Carruthers shook his head. 'I don't think so for a moment, but naturally he'll make himself a nuisance because he's worried about his daughter . . . '

A grave-faced manservant showed them out, and fifteen minutes later they were seated at a corner table in a quiet café, all three of them unusually thoughtful. To Garth and Whittaker in particular the afternoon had been one of amazing revelations. Carruthers, for his part, was no longer musing on the mechanics of the Kestrel case: his active brain was grappling with other profound problems that had been laid in his lap.

'I'm worried,' Garth confessed at length, hiccupping over his cup of tea. 'Everything is more or less sorted out except the problem of where Vera *is*. If only I could nail her — or Alroyd. The bank could put things straight, but they won't divulge a thing — certainly not who Leslie Gantry is.'

'The bank is hardly likely to know anyway,' Carruthers shrugged. 'What you can do though is have the Assistant Commissioner notify all banks that Leslie Gantry is required by Scotland Yard to answer certain questions concerning Vera de Maine-Kestrel. I think you'll find that will do it. By this time Vera will have fitted herself into the role of Leslie Gantry, and she can't *withdraw* from that role. Faced with the issue of having to talk about Vera she'll either have to stop using her bank account as Leslie Gantry and drop from sight — which she won't do. I think, since she loves money; or else she'll have to come forward and speak. Alroyd will fit in automatically once you get Vera taped. No use looking for Alroyd: his name will be different, and you don't even know what he looks like. The other move I'd suggest is that you tackle Sidney Laycock and somehow throw a scare into him. Get to know from him *why* Vera went through all this elaborate planning. If you don't feel you can break him down leave him to me: I'll make him think he's facing Lucifer himself!'

'You serious?' Garth asked. 'I mean about tackling him?'

'Of course! I love insulting people — as maybe you've noticed.'

'That being the case,' Garth said, 'I'll make arrangements for him to be at the Yard this evening. Seven-thirty — our favorite time. How would that suit you?'

'Excellently,' Carruthers assented.

★   ★   ★

Garth was as good as his word, and exactly at 7.30 Sidney Laycock, not looking at all happy, presented himself a few minutes in precedence of Carruthers. The glint in the little physicist's eyes was sufficient indication that he meant business, and Garth was perfectly prepared to let him have his fling, mainly because not being an official of the law Carruthers was not tied down by rules and regulations and could accuse, slang, or, if need be compliment, exactly as he saw fit.

'You don't know me, do you?' Carruthers asked bluntly, tossing down his homburg onto the desk and sprawling in the armchair.

'Afraid not,' Laycock responded, then some of his habitual impudence came to his rescue as he added: 'unless you're the man perpetuated in busts in musical salons.'

Whittaker, in charge of an unnoticed tape recorder that was taking down the entire interview, grinned to himself whilst Garth cleared his throat noisily.

'I know I look like Beethoven,' Carruthers shrugged. 'And I have similar genius — in a different way. I am a scientist, Mr. Laycock, and as such am in a position to bring you to justice any moment I choose. Whether I do so or not depends on how you behave this evening.'

'Since you are not an official member of the police I don't have to respond to anything you may ask of me,' Laycock retorted.

'Don't adopt that tone to me, young man, or I may become really nasty! For your own sake you'll tell me everything I wish to know. If you don't comply your arrest for the murder — even the dismemberment — of Vera de Maine-Kestrel will immediately follow. That quite clear?'

Laycock shifted uncomfortably in his chair and gave a sullen glance of acquiescence.

'Good! Very well then, as a scientist I have all the legal proof that you murdered Vera de Maine-Kestrel, using a knife and a hacksaw for dismemberment, afterwards destroying the remains in a bath of nitric acid. You overlooked a gold tooth-shell, which has been identified by the dental surgeon concerned as belonging to the late Vera. Frankly, Mr. Laycock, the forensic department and I have piled up such a mass of evidence against you you're caught like a rat in a trap.'

'I *didn't* kill Vera!' Laycock shouted hotly, perspiration gleaming on his forehead. 'I swear I haven't seen her since the day she disappeared — or rather the evening. I don't know a single thing about the business. Everything has been *planted* on me!'

'Planted?' Carruthers raised a cynical eyebrow. 'Why on earth should it be? The only person who would be likely to plant anything would be the unfortunate Vera herself, and she would not have the remotest reason to do so. No, Mr. Laycock, none of that holds water. Now there are other things which make your conviction for her murder absolutely certain — '

'She *could* have had a reason!' Laycock broke in desperately.

'Don't interrupt,' Caruthers snapped. 'As I was saying — Mmmm, *what* did you say? Vera could have had a *reason?* What, for instance?'

Laycock breathed hard and lighted a cigarette with a shaky hand.

'I suppose, if it comes to it, that the sentence for blackmail is less severe than for murder, so to save myself I'd better give you my side of it.'

Carruthers and Garth exchanged a brief glance.

'Let's hear it,' Garth ordered. 'And don't expect us to instantly believe you, either. You had the chance to speak long ago, and didn't.'

'What has happened to Vera I don't know,' Laycock went on, 'but evidently it is time I mentioned that our intended marriage was not born of romance but of necessity. It was cold-blooded, commercial proposition. We didn't love each other one jot.'

'So I've gathered,' Garth remarked. 'Keep on talking.'

'If Vera married me she stood to save thousands of pounds. Until we *were* married I forced her to pay me a considerable sum every month to keep my mouth shut. Over a period of four years, when she first had to start paying me, she's parted with quite a few thousands. I was going to bring the payments to an end when she married me. I considered it worth it: I would get an attractive girl and would be able to force her to settle a considerable sum on me. And she wouldn't be able to refuse.'

'Because of Michael Ayrton?' Carruthers asked, with a bleak stare.

'You know about that, then? Inspector Garth here mentioned Ayrton's name to me once and that was when I knew he was on to something.'

'Go on explaining yourself,' Carruthers ordered.

'I knew Michael Ayrton very well, and I was present in his flat on the evening he was murdered. Matter of fact I was in an adjoining room, half asleep, recovering from a bout of excess drinking. I saw Vera with him, and I also saw her leave after she had defended herself against Ayrton's drunken advances. She used the heavy metal firestand as a weapon to scare him off, but did not use it. When she had gone Ayrton, too tight to stand straight, fell over the rug and went his length, striking his head violently on the firestand and, as events showed later, killing himself. I took the firestand away with me since it had Vera's fingerprints on it and, had I given it to the police, she'd have been convicted of murder for certain. I'd always fancied her wealth, however — and, in a way, her herself — so I made myself attentive to her and, as the police were stumped for definite evidence in the Ayrton case and could not convict her, I told her of the firestand carefully put away which, if produced, could put a rope round her neck. What more natural than that she paid up to keep me quiet?'

'You have the firestand even yet?' Carruthers questioned.

'Safely put away, yes, and I took good care never to smudge it.'

'Very well. If you can produce that it can be traced back to the Ayrton flat your story will hold water. So you blackmailed Vera, only consenting to stop bleeding her white when you were married?'

'That's it — but in the meantime I believe she evolved a plan to have a double purpose. One, to disappear and get away from me; and two, make it look as though I'd murdered her. I am convinced that is the solution. That's all I have to say, and you can call me a skunk if you like.'

'I will, with pleasure,' Carruthers said coldly. 'Best thing you can do, Garth, is book him for blackmail and let the law take its course.'

'You can hardly do that when everything shows Vera is dead,' Laycock retorted. 'My own confession to blackmail won't hold in a court of law without Vera herself to accuse me.'

'That can probably be arranged,' Carruthers said dryly. 'We do not believe Vera *is* dead, Mr. Laycock. I spun you a yarn just to soften you up. Candidly, the evidences showing how you 'murdered' her wouldn't convince a child of two, let alone a learned judge who knows all the answers.'

Laycock stared, then his cheeks coloured darkly with anger.

'You mean to tell *me* — '

'Yes,' Garth said sourly. 'And I'm doing as Dr. Carruthers suggests, charging you with blackmail on your own confession — which has been tape-recorded over there. Later, Vera herself may be in a position to prefer charges against you. It even looks as though I've managed to solve the Ayrton case as well as the Kestrel one, which is all to the good.'

Cornered, Laycock did not say any more. The charge against him complete he was presently escorted from the office and Carruthers spread his hands.

'A classic example of leading up the garden path. And, incidentally, did you adopt my suggestion of asking the A.C. to notify all banks that Leslie Gantry is wanted by Scotland Yard?'

'I did,' Garth assented. 'All we can do now is wait and see what happens. Meantime, doctor, many thanks indeed for your scientific help. I'll let you know how the rest of it works out.'

'So I should hope,' Carruthers grinned, getting to his feet. 'I'd rather hoped myself that — '

He broke off as a constable appeared in the doorway.

'There's a lady to see you, Inspector. She won't give her name but says it is very urgent.'

'What's she look like?' Garth questioned.

'Hard to tell, sir. She's wearing one of those old-fashioned veil things. Her whole set-up is pretty Spanish, if you ask me, but her English is good enough. She said she hardly expected to find you here at this time but decided to take a chance.'

'All right,' Garth sighed. 'Show her in . . .'

The constable departed, and Carruthers buttoned up his huge overcoat.

'Won't be anything in this for me, Garth, so I'll be on my way. Let me know how things work out.'

Garth nodded, and at that moment the unknown woman came in at the doorway, preventing Carruthers from leaving. She seemed to give a quick glance about her behind the veil, then she lifted it.

'This is either coincidence gone mad,' Garth said slowly, 'or else you are Vera de Maine-Kestrel!'

'She is!' Whittaker confirmed flatly. 'Despite her black hair.'

'Yes, gentlemen,' Vera said quietly. 'Quite correct . . .'

She looked uncertainly about her then took the chair Carruthers proffered. He stood waiting interestedly. Whittaker, knowing the girl from the bright young thing she had been was struggling now to fathom this sober young woman who looked as if she were carrying a mountain of responsibility.

'I thought it better to come back home and make a clean breast of everything than be murdered,' she said quietly, after a long interval.

'Murdered?' Garth's eyebrows rose.

'By the man with whom I ran away to Spain — Bob Alroyd. I found out a plot he had worked out by which I'd settle a considerable sum of money on him — two hundred thousand pounds to be exact — and then meet with an accident. It's my own fault. I should have known that a man who'll murder once will do it again. It wasn't me he wanted. It was my money.'

'You seem to be unfortunate in your choice of lovers,' Carruthers commented dryly. 'And allow me to introduce myself. I am Doctor Hiram Carruthers, scientific specialist to Scotland Yard, and the man who unraveled the complicated web surrounding your disappearance.'

Vera looked at him in surprise. 'You don't mean you actually found the method used by Bob Alroyd to make me disappear?'

'I did — and I'm glad you've admitted that *he* thought of it.'

'Our side of the business can come later,' Garth said. 'We want certain verification from you first, Miss Kestrel. So you made a gataway to Spain, after having first arranged for two hundred and fifty thousand pounds to be placed to the credit of Leslie Gantry — Leslie Gantry being you. That it?'

'Well, yes. But how do you know?'

'Purely a matter of deduction. At this moment all major banks are on the lookout for Leslie Gantry, but that can now be withdrawn since you've come back of your own accord. You left to avoid blackmail of Sidney Laycock for the Ayrton case — in which you have now been proven innocent — and the black mark against you is that you tried to get

Laycock accused of your murder!'

'That was Bob's doing,' Vera said seriously. 'My idea was simply to disappear and escape the blackmailing, but Bob said my proposition didn't go half far enough, and he worked out the whole scheme of my grand exit by 'magical' means and also set the stage for Sidney to take the blame for my murder. I suppose I was a fool to obey Bob's orders so completely, but I hadn't much choice. He just ran things, and used my money to do it.'

'But surely you went to Laycock's laboratory and left your clothes?' Garth questioned.

'Yes. I left clothes and fingerprints, as Bob had told me to do. The worst part was having to gash myself with a hacksaw, but I went through with it. I got a key impression from Sidney long ago — in a piece of soap as a matter of fact when, one evening, he'd left his blazer in the pavilion with the laboratory key in it. I knew it well enough.'

'In other words you were an unwilling party to your own disappearance?' Carruthers asked.

'Not to my disappearance — to the deliberate misrepresentation of my murder. But if I did not agree to that Bob would not have helped me to escape Sidney's blackmailing, and Bob insisted that the only safe way to kill the blackmailing was to wipe out the blackmailer. If, on the clues provided, the police thought he'd done away with me, all well and good . . . Later, I was horrified to learn that Crafto, whom I'd paid well to keep the vanishing act a dead secret, had been murdered. Bob never admitted that he killed Crafto, but I'm pretty sure he did. I remember he was late joining me after I'd made my quick change at Sidney's laboratory, and he also seemed pretty anxious to be away . . . Well, away we got, to our pre-arranged destination in Spain, and once there I realized Bob was not all he seemed to be.'

'That he was just another fortune hunter, and a murderer to boot?' Garth suggested.

'Yes. As I say, I realized that, no matter what the consequences, I must come back home and explain. I must have been crazy anyway to ever indulge in such a mad escapade. Only I was scared of Sidney and willing to try anything to get away from him and the constant possibility of being accused of murdering Michael Ayrton.'

'You can forget all that,' Garth said. 'Laycock will not trouble you again. Our task now is to get Robert Alroyd. Where was he when you left him?'

'In Spain — Madrid.' Vera opened her handbag and handed over a printed card. 'This is the hotel where we checked in, and from which I vanished this afternoon by the first available plane when I knew what Bob was getting at.'

'Have you a photograph of him?' Garth questioned.

'I have this, in my wrist-locket.' Vera fiddled with the solid gold chain bracelet about her wrist and opened the heart that depended from it. From within she pulled out a tiny photograph, but it was nevertheless clear enough.

'This will do,' Garth nodded. 'The long arm will reach out and seize Robert Alroyd, Miss Kestrel — have no doubts as to that. As far as you yourself are concerned, you will sign a statement stating exactly what happened from the very start of your escapade, and then you will be called as a witness when Alroyd is brought for trial. Whether or not the judge is stern or lenient in view of your behavior I cannot say, but the fact would seem to be that you have been exploited by two completely ruthless men, chiefly because of your wealth, and at a young age you have learned by bitter experience that the world can be a very unpleasant place sometimes.'

'Can — can I go home, then?' Vera asked quickly. 'Can I see Dad and take a load off his mind?'

'Certainly — but don't leave town until I say so. A full statement will be brought to your home tomorrow for you to sign, and it will include our own findings for your verification. Finally, Miss Kestrel, I would say this: In deciding to come home and make a clean breast of things you have revealed sound commonsense. I am sure that when the trial comes up the judge will take that into full account . . . '